Murder, Of Course

A Sugarbury Falls Mystery

by

Diane Weiner

For information, email Cozy Cat Press, cozycatpress@aol.com or visit our website at: www.cozycatpress.com

COZY CAT
P R E S S

ISBN: 978-1-946063-47-2

Printed in the United States of America

Cover design by Paula Ellenberger
www.paulaellenberger.com

10 9 8 7 6 5 4 3 2 1

This book is dedicated to cat lovers everywhere!

Chapter 1

Emily bolted upright, gasping as she pulled the quilt up to her neck. Chester meowed and darted off the bed like a black bullet. She shook her husband. "Henry, someone's pounding on our door. Get up."

Henry groaned. "What? Who's knocking at this hour? They're going to wake up Maddy."

"Come on." Her bare feet swung over the bed and she winced when they made contact with the frigid wooden floor. She grabbed her velour robe. "Alright, already. Stop pounding. We're coming." She climbed down the rungs of their loft bedroom ladder after her husband, nearly losing her footing in the dim light.

"Emily, Henry, open up. It's an emergency."

Henry felt the night air on his cheeks when he opened the door and came face to face with his flannel-clad neighbor, Kurt Olav.

"Kurt, what's wrong?" Having never seen this Minnesota to Vermont transplant rattled, Henry knew by his neighbor's uneasy demeanor that something was seriously awry.

"I was walking Prancer, and I stopped by the cabin I bought for Chloe. You know, the one I'm renting while she finishes grad school. The young lady who's renting it moved in a few days ago. She...she called last night to tell me the porch light was out. I grabbed a new bulb, figuring I'd pop it in this morning." Prancer pulled against his leash.

"And?" Emily closed her robe tighter.

Kurt fidgeted as if it would make his words come out faster. "It was still dark out, but her lights were on, so I figured she was up. Then I knocked to let her know I was fixing it. When she didn't answer, I...I peeked through the open curtain and she's laying on the floor, not moving, you know, still—like she's hurt or something. I used my key, ran inside, and I think...something's not right. Come on, Henry. You're a doctor, come help."

"Did you call 911?" asked Henry.

"I don't have my phone on me."

Henry grabbed his keys and they piled into his car, while Emily called 911. Prancer, the chocolate lab, hopped on Kurt's lap. Henry sped past their barn, behind Kurt's place, and around the back of his property to a small Lincoln-log style cabin. Kurt and Prancer jumped out of the Jeep before Henry had a chance to turn off the engine and made a beeline for the door.

"See, there she is. She's not moving, like I told you." Kurt pointed to the floor.

Henry knelt down next to the woman, feeling for a pulse. "She's not breathing." He looked around the tiny living area. "Keep the door open for when the paramedics get here." Prancer stood guard on the porch, a trusty sentinel ready to signal the ambulance.

"She's...she's not dead, is she? She can't be dead." Emily paced back and forth, questions racing through her head. *Who is she? Where's she from? She's young. There isn't any blood. What happened to her?* It felt like deja-vu. She'd been through this before, just last winter when her co-worker was murdered, and again last summer with the biker.

"Kurt, was the door locked when you found her?" Henry stood up.

"Yeah. Like I said, I used my key."

"She's wearing jeans and a sweat shirt. Looks like this happened before she went to bed."

Emily went into the kitchen area. "There's a bowl in the sink, and a pot of cold soup on the stove. One spoon and one glass. Poor thing was alone when this happened."

Henry said, "Could be an underlying medical condition like diabetes—or a heart issue."

A wisp of blond hair matted against the girl's forehead made Emily's newly discovered maternal instincts kick in. "Her hair is the same color as Maddy's. I wish the ambulance would hurry. Her poor parents."

Prancer barked. "I hear sirens," said Kurt. The paramedics rushed in. "She's over there."

Kneeling beside her, one of the EMTs searched for a pulse, while the other set up the portable defibrillator.

"She wasn't breathing when we found her," said Henry. "I'm afraid you're too late."

When the paramedics were satisfied that Henry's observation was correct, they lifted her onto the metal stretcher. "What's her name?"

"I... we...don't know." Emily spotted the woman's purse on the floor in front of the sofa and pulled out a wallet. "Danielle LaPierre. From Falls Church, Virginia. We'll follow you to the hospital."

The sun had just begun to rise above the mountains. On the way to the Jeep, Henry picked up a piece of thick, dew-covered plastic from the grass just beyond the porch.

"Kurt, do you know what this is from?"

"It's sealant. Plugs up the drafts. I prefer good old-fashioned weather stripping myself."

Henry wondered what it was doing in the yard, especially since, despite the chillier nights and mornings, it was technically still summer. Kurt always did his own repairs, and he just said he preferred weather stripping, so why was it lying on the lawn?

They dropped Prancer off at Kurt's, then continued to the regional hospital. Once inside, they waited for Pat Hester, the medical examiner and Henry's best friend, to give them a preliminary cause of death.

"What's taking your buddy so long?" asked Kurt. "Why don't you go in there and hurry him up?"

"Pat's thorough. He'll take his time making sure all the *i*'s are dotted and the *t*'s are crossed. If he suspects foul play, he won't tell us anything unless he's sure."

Emily sank into the plastic chair in the waiting room, wondering if Maddy was awake yet. She sent her a text to let her know they were at the hospital. She and Henry were new to parenting, having become recent guardians of a fourteen-year old when Emily's former college roommate had died suddenly. Kurt paced, and Henry checked his phone. It seemed as if hours had gone by. Emily considered going home, just as the town's two best detectives, Megan O'Leary and Ron Wooster, walked into the waiting room.

"Detectives? Does that mean this was a murder?" said Emily, addressing no one in particular, but within earshot of Kurt and her husband.

"We investigate whenever there's an unexplained death. Just following protocol."

Detective O'Leary was about the same age as her partner—mid-thirties—both talented cops who'd risen quickly through the ranks. "Can you tell us how you discovered the body?"

Kurt stood up. "Last night, the new tenant called to say the front light was out, so this morning, I dropped by to replace it. It wasn't yet dawn, but all the lights were on, so I knocked on the door. When I didn't get an answer, I peeked through the open curtains and saw the girl sprawled on the floor. I didn't have my phone, so I ran over to Henry's, since he's a doctor, and brought him and Emily over. Henry said she was dead."

"I checked for a pulse, and she wasn't breathing."

"We called the paramedics on the way to the cabin," said Emily.

Pat came through the door of the waiting room. Acknowledging the detectives and his friends, he stated, "I have to wait for test results, but it looks like carbon monoxide poisoning."

"Carbon monoxide? How's that possible?" said Kurt.

"One of the appliances may have been faulty. Perhaps the hot water heater. She wasn't grilling indoors, was she?"

"No, of course not. And I keep those appliances in good repair. Don't go telling me this was my fault."

Detective Wooster finished typing into his iPad. "No one's saying it's your fault, Mr. Olav. I understand you found her ID?"

Emily pulled the wallet out of her purse. "Her name is Danielle LaPierre, from Falls Church, Virginia."

"Thank you. We'll notify the next of kin. We went over to the cabin, and we called the crime scene unit from Burlington. They have more advanced equipment than we've got here."

"Crime scene?" said Emily.

"Just a precaution. Go on home," said Detective O'Leary. "There's nothing you can do here."

Back in the Jeep, Emily checked her texts. "Maddy must still be asleep."

Henry had a thought. "Do you want to stop at the Outside Inn and grab breakfast? We can bring home some pancakes for Maddy."

"I guess so," said Emily. "I was going to take Maddy shopping for school clothes, but the stores aren't even open yet."

Kurt agreed that breakfast sounded like a good idea. "I don't get it. Carbon monoxide? Those appliances are in tip-top shape. I bought the place for my daughter. You know I put in the best for Chloe. Wasn't expecting to have to rent it out to a stranger. If she smelled gas, why didn't this girl get on out of there, or call me?"

"You can't smell carbon monoxide," said Henry. "The stove she was cooking on was electric, wasn't it?"

"Yeah. I replaced the old gas stove as soon as I bought the place."

Emily said, "What about the pot-bellied stove? Or the water heater?"

"I checked everything myself before I rented it out. I don't get it. They better not try and pin this on me."

"No one's saying it's your fault, Kurt." Henry pulled into the bed and breakfast. "It's a horrible tragedy, but accidents happen. Don't blame yourself." He pulled in front of a yellow inn with white shutters and a wrap-around porch. "Let's eat."

Emily salivated at the aroma of fresh cinnamon rolls that met her at the door. Coralee, the sparkly-eyed, gray-haired owner, came out from behind the desk.

"You're up bright and early. Come on in. The specialty this morning is blueberry French toast." She led them into the dining room, where a few vacationers were already eating. "What are you all doing up so early on a Saturday morning?"

Emily said, "To make a long story short, a few days ago, Kurt rented out the place he bought for his daughter, Chloe. This morning, he found the tenant dead on the cabin floor. They say it was carbon monoxide poisoning."

"Those appliances in the place were all working fine. She must have fooled with them some way," said Kurt.

"How awful! It was the pretty, blond lawyer, wasn't it?"

"A lawyer? I don't know, but she was pretty and blond. You know her?"

"Yeah, Em. She was staying here. Said she was looking for a longer term rental. I was surprised, since summer season is coming to an end, and the foliage seekers aren't due for another month. She said she was here on business and it might take a while to see it through. I sent her Kurt's way since I knew Chloe had decided to go out of town for grad school. She moved out of here just a few days ago."

"Thanks for the referral," said Kurt. With his dry personality, Emily couldn't tell whether or not Kurt was being sincere, or sarcastic.

"That was her, then. Danielle LaPierre," said Henry.

"Yeah, that was her name—Danielle. Noah noticed her right away. That boy of mine has an eye for beauty and smarts. Can't believe she's dead, God bless her soul." She made the sign of the cross.

"Did she mention any family?" asked Emily.

"She said her parents were celebrating their fortieth anniversary and were taking a world cruise. I thought that was pretty neat."

"They will be devastated when they get the news," said Emily.

"Now that you're a parent, can you even imagine?" said Coralee.

"I'd be destroyed if anything happened to Maddy. So would Henry." Henry nodded in agreement.

"Speaking of being a parent, Maddy seems to be adjusting well. Are you thinking of adopting her?"

"Fiona named me legal guardian in her will but it's only been a few months. I don't want to push Maddy. She's still coping with her mother's death."

"She's lucky to have you both. I'm sure she'll love Sugarbury High."

"We're going back to school shopping later, for both of us! I start teaching my classes at St. Edwards soon. The summer flew by."

"I'll get your food going. French toast all around?"

"Sounds good," said Henry. "And pack up a to-go plate for Maddy."

Chapter 2

As soon as they got home, Emily checked the kitchen. "She's not in here."

"She's not in here, either." Henry gently opened the guest bedroom door on the other side of the living room. *Guest bedroom—he'd have to stop calling it that.* It was Maddy's room now. Maddy was snuggled up with Chester. She opened her eyes when the door creaked.

"I didn't mean to wake you. We just got back from the hospital and I wanted to make sure you were okay."

"The hospital?" Maddy picked up her phone from the night stand.

"Kurt's tenant. I'll explain over breakfast. We brought you some of Coralee's French toast."

Maddy sleepily pulled on a plaid robe dusted with black cat fur that had belonged to her mother. She scooped up Chester and followed Henry into the kitchen.

"There you are. Did you get my text?" Emily poured water into the coffeemaker.

"What text?"

"Em, she just now woke up."

Emily couldn't help glancing at the rooster-shaped clock on the wall. It was nearly noon and she worried Maddy wouldn't be able to wake up early once school started.

"I thought after breakfast we could ride over to the outlet mall," said Emily. "Did you make a list of what you need in the way of school clothes like I asked?"

Maddy picked at her breakfast. "No, not yet. Just some jeans and a few shirts I guess."

"We don't have much time left for shopping. I have to go in this week and set up my writing class at the college, and next weekend is Labor Day. Then it's back to school for both of us."

Henry, noticing Maddy's reticence, said, "The first day's the hardest. Once you get in there and see what it's like, I'm sure you'll make new friends."

"We can stop at the Sugar-buried Shoppe while we're there," said Emily. Her phone vibrated. "It's a text from the new department chair at St. Edwards. She says she expected to have my syllabus on her desk by now. If I don't send it to her by the end of the day, she'll make one for me. What? I haven't even met her yet and already I don't like her."

Henry said, "She's probably just feeling the pressure of starting the new semester. Everyone loved your summer class—you know what you're doing."

"Still, I don't appreciate the tone. Like I haven't made a syllabus."

"We don't need the money. You can stay home and concentrate on writing your next book if you want. When you retired from the newspaper, you weren't planning on another stressful career."

"Yeah, but I can't even collect social security for another decade. I feel like I should still be contributing to society, you know? Besides, I haven't gotten an inspiration for my next book yet."

Maddy said, "Tell me what happened this morning? Who died?"

"Kurt rented out his daughter's cabin to a young lawyer. This morning when he peeked in, the tenant was dead! Apparently she died from carbon monoxide poisoning. Kurt says he checked all the appliances and everything was in working order."

"There you go. That sounds like a true crime book to me," said Maddy.

"Maddy, a woman is dead. And no one said anything about it being a crime."

"We can assume it was an accident unless proven otherwise," said Henry. "How's the French toast?" Henry himself wasn't convinced the girl's death was an accident.

After breakfast, Maddy pulled on a pair of denim shorts and grabbed her meager list.

Emily cleared the breakfast dishes and said, "Henry, are you sure you don't want to come along?"

She needed Henry beside her, though she'd never come out and say it directly. She was afraid of saying the wrong thing, of being too overbearing, or not confident enough in dealing with Maddy. She'd watched enough TV to know clothing is a ripe battleground between parents and teens. Did she just say parents? Some days she felt like Maddy's parent; other days she felt like an imposter and worried about scarring Maddy for life by saying the wrong thing or giving poor advice. She'd certainly failed in taking care of her own sister.

"No, I have a few things to do. I'm almost finished making Maddy's bookshelf. She'll need it for when school starts." Henry had converted the barn into a woodworking studio shortly after they inherited his parents' cabin last year. Besides, he was hoping Pat would get back to him with more details about the dead lawyer after he completed the autopsy. He loved a good puzzle.

Emily and Maddy headed to the outlet mall. The lush, green trees would soon be changing color and Emily couldn't wait. They'd moved to Vermont at the tail end of the season last year. Fall was her favorite time of the year. With the days growing shorter and the crops dying off, many found the end of summer to be depressing. To her, it was a new beginning—a new school year for Maddy, a new semester for her at St. Edwards, and hopefully, the beginning of her next true crime book. This, she was struggling with. The harder she strained to find an idea, the more elusive it was.

"What do you think happened to that lady they found in Kurt's rental cottage?" said Maddy. Like Emily, she and Henry shared a love of mysteries.

"So far, they know it's carbon monoxide poisoning, but Kurt swears all the appliances were in good working order. I think he had to have overlooked something. I'm not saying it's his fault or anything. I just don't have another explanation."

"Where was she from?"

"Virginia. She was looking for a short term rental."

Maddy spit out a stream of questions. "Why was she up here? Didn't Henry say she was a lawyer? Didn't she have a job back home? A short term rental sounds like a vacation, not work. From what I've heard, lawyers, especially when they're starting out, work like dogs."

"Those are good questions. We don't yet know what her specialty was."

"Any new criminal cases around here?" she asked casually, as if she was asking what was for dinner that night. "She could be a defense lawyer...for a murderer."

"New criminal cases? This is a safe little town." She watched Maddy's expression. "Okay, so the biker was an exception."

Maddy said, "What was her name again? I'll google her. Falls Church, right?"

"Yes, and it's Danielle LaPierre. D-A-N..."

"I can spell Danielle. And it's L-A-P..."

"Okay, okay. Go for it." She wondered how Maddy's phone always had service, when her own was spotty at best.

After a few minutes, Maddy said, "Got it. She's an estate lawyer. Maybe one of the residents is going to inherit some money."

"Well, I know for sure it isn't me or Henry." She was amazed Maddy had found the information so quickly. Henry was right. Maddy was both intelligent and inquisitive. He couldn't believe how fast she'd gotten the hang of the Sudoku puzzles he was so fond of. She wondered if Sugarbury High had gifted classes—was it too late to get her in? Did they still *have* gifted classes?

They came around a bend and the outlet mall was in full view. Emily parked as close to the American Eagle and Pink outlets as she could. Would Maddy need a backpack? A tote? The Coach outlet was at the other end of the mall.

Maddy said, "American Eagle has nice jeans. Mom used to take me there for back to school shopping in Chicago."

"You got those shorts you're wearing in that store last time we were here, remember?"

"Yeah." She followed Emily into the mall. Back to school sales were running rampant, even at the outlets. Maddy rifled through the jeans.

Emily felt awkward. She didn't even know what size Maddy wore. She pulled a few cute tops from the rack. "Do you like these?"

"They're okay. I'm going to try these on." She headed toward the dressing room with an armful of pants, ignoring the bundle in Emily's arms. She was once again overthinking the whole parenting thing, when a colleague from school came up beside her.

"Emily, back to school shopping? I've already spent a small fortune on my daughter."

Emily wondered how much was considered a fortune. She had no idea what the average parent should spend on back to school shopping. "Maddy's in the fitting room. I haven't been back to school shopping since my own senior year in high school. I hope Maddy adjusts to her new school. Her middle school back in Chicago was three times the size of Sugarbury High."

Nancy said, "It's easier going from big to small than the other way around. She'll be fine. Are you ready to start the new semester?"

"I'm looking forward to it. I've spent all summer designing my new course. By the way, have you met our new department chair?"

"Mair Rose? Yeah, I met her. I brought some new office supplies over the other day and she was strolling the halls with her clipboard and checklist. Walked right past me when I said hello. Looks like a witch with jet black hair and pasty skin."

"I wasn't crazy about her tone in an email she sent me. Too bad Shera went and got herself that assistant dean job at Boston U. I liked her a lot."

"Everyone did."

A freckled blond in distressed jeans and a shirt that barely grazed her belt said, "Mom, can I get both of these and the sweatshirt?"

"How much?" said Nancy. She searched for the price tags. "Okay, but our shopping budget is now officially exhausted. Brooke, this is Emily Fox. Her office is next to mine. Her daughter, Maddy, will be starting school with you."

Maddy came out of the dressing room.

"How'd those work out?" said Emily.

"They're good."

"Maddy, this is my colleague, Nancy Patterson, and her daughter…"

"Brooke. Hey, I have those same jeans. Your Mom says you'll be starting school with me."

Emily felt that familiar shiver, part excitement, part fight or flight, whenever someone referred to her as Maddy's mother.

Maddy glanced at the floor, then up at Brooke. "I'll be there."

Brooke handed Maddy her phone. "Put in your number. We have a group chat going and this way you'll feel like you know some people before you start."

Emily said, "Isn't that sweet." She gulped when she realized she sounded like her own grandmother making a comment like that.

Nancy said, "We're going to head home now that the money's all spent. I'll see you Monday, Emily."

Chapter 3

Henry took advantage of his free Saturday by catching up with his pal Pat over lunch at The Outside Inn. He was glad Emily hadn't objected to his bowing out of back to school shopping. Succumbing to Maddy's influence, Henry ordered a grilled veggie sandwich; Pat went for the burger and fries.

"Doesn't looking at clogged arteries and fatty livers down at the morgue convince you to eat healthier?"

"Just the opposite. Reminds me life is short. Eat burgers. Drink beer while you're at it." He raised his beer stein in a toast. "I hate drinking alone. Come on; we're both off duty."

"Maybe just one." He motioned to the waitress and ordered a pumpkin craft beer. "Any more news on the dead lawyer?"

"Carbon monoxide level was sky high, even for an accidental death."

"What are you saying?"

"It had to be deliberate."

"And this is you talking, or your girlfriend the detective?"

"Both. Megan said the fireplace was blocked."

"You mean, like stuffed with leaves?"

"No, Kurt had a chimney sweep in there right after he bought the place. It was intentional. Chimney was stuffed with old clothing."

"Really? That's hard to believe." Henry had a sudden thought. "I hope whoever it was wasn't after Chloe. If they find out they missed…"

"Chloe's safely away at graduate school. We know nothing about the lawyer. Who knows what enemies she had?"

The waitress brought lunch to the table. Henry's mind sped through the possibilities. Young, pretty lawyer...jealous boyfriend, deranged husband...estate deal gone wrong...

Pat said, "You saw the victim. Did you notice anything unusual at all?"

"Like I told your girlfriend, I found a piece of plastic foam on the front lawn. Kurt said he was planning to seal the cracks but not for a few weeks yet."

"Megan asked me if the victim smoked. They found an empty cigarette pack outside by the trash can. I did the autopsy myself and the victim was definitely not a smoker. And I know Kurt doesn't smoke."

A chatty group of three, two women and a man, entered the restaurant area wearing identical long sleeved t-shirts. They were of similar ages and both of the women had handbags shaped like cats. Coralee seated them near the window.

"Tourists," said Pat.

"All wearing *I Love my Cat* t-shirts? That's just, well, just weird."

Coralee stopped at their table on her way back out to the lobby.

"Boy's day out? I heard Emily say she was taking Maddy to the outlet mall this weekend."

"Yep. Emily is hoping some retail therapy might cheer Maddy up about starting school. She's missing her friends back in Chicago."

"Poor girl. Starting high school is tough enough but in a new place where you don't know any of the other kids? It was a tough time for Noah and he grew up here."

Henry said, "What do you mean?" He knew Noah had some brushes with the law, but knew little about his earlier years.

"You know, high school can be very cliquey, especially in a small town like this. Noah always felt like an outsider." She looked at Henry's worried expression. "Not to say Maddy will have trouble. Noah marches to the beat of his own drummer. I'm sure Maddy will fit in just fine."

Henry hoped that would be true, however, in the short time they'd been Maddy's guardians, he knew she was no ordinary cookie. She was exceptionally bright, and didn't buy into a lot of mainstream ideas. She'd rather sit in her room with a book than spend hours on––what was it she thought was a waste of time? Snap Chat, that was it. And how many of her classmates wouldn't think she was weird for eating tofu instead of cheeseburgers?

Pat chugged the remainder of his beer. "Coralee, what's with the cat ladies over by the window?"

"Haven't you seen the local news? Final auditions for a national cat food commercial are taking place right here in our little old town. It's sponsored by that cat food company, Feline Feast out of Burlington. The winning cat gets to be the face of the company, and the owner gets a half a million-dollar prize... plus free cat food for life."

Pat laughed. "So it's the cat equivalent of America's Got Talent?"

"No," laughed Henry. "America's Next Runway Cat Model."

"Laugh all you want, boys. It's bringing lots of business to the inn and to the town in general. Hey, Sugarbury Falls even got a mention on the national news."

Pat turned to Henry. "We should run down to the shelter and adopt ourselves some contenders. There's a project for your daughter."

Henry found himself liking the word *daughter*. "She's excellent with Chester."

Pat said, "Eureka. She should enter him."

Coralee shook her head. "Hate to burst your bubble, boys, but that ship has sailed. The company's been having mass auditions all year in cities across the country."

"You mean like a cattle call?" said Pat

"No, a cat call," said Henry. "I wasn't far off with the runway reference."

"Knock it off, boys. You can laugh all you want, but only four finalists were chosen and there they are."

"I count three," said Pat.

"Unfortunately, Danielle, God rest her soul, is no longer with us. Her cat, Max, was one of the finalists."

Henry's phone vibrated. "It's Emily. She and Maddy are on their way home."

"How about some dessert before you go?" said Coralee.

"I'll take a slice of your blueberry pie," said Pat.

"Ditto," said Henry. "And another beer."

Chapter 4

When Henry drove into his driveway, Emily's car wasn't yet in its spot. He seized the opportunity to work on Maddy's bookshelf in the barn he'd converted to a woodworking shop. He wondered if someday the shelf might be handed down to Maddy's child—his grandchild. He had abandoned the idea of having children when he'd decided he wanted to spend his life with Emily, who was firmly opposed to having children. Truthfully, it had barely phased him. Growing up an only child, he was close to his parents and considered himself lucky not having to share his things and put up with the household chaos like his friends with siblings did. Why had Maddy coming into his life changed all this?

He sanded the freshly cut wood and was about to start applying primer when Kurt knocked on the barn door and slid it open.

"You work fast. Last week when I came by you were just starting." Prancer licked Henry's arm.

"I love working with my hands. This gave me a project to focus on. I couldn't decide whether to paint it white, or just stain it, but the primer sort of flew into my hands." He didn't say how he pictured a little granddaughter coming to visit and how he would fill it with science books, and maybe those Encyclopedia Brown mysteries he used to love as a child. He imagined Emily stenciling roses or Maddy's name along the side of it.

"I just got a weird call from some cat groomer. Said she'd been trying to get in touch with Ms. LaPierre and she'd given my number as an emergency contact."

"Emergency contact for a groomer? That doesn't sound right."

"Danielle left a cat with her. Said something about getting it ready for his big debut, whatever that means. Anyhow, she wants to know what to do with it. She doesn't have room to keep boarding him."

Henry put the pieces together. "Coralee said Danielle was in town for some bigtime cat commercial. There were three entrants at the inn having lunch."

"Cat commercial?" Kurt winced.

"Don't get me started." He heard Emily's car pull into the driveway. "They're home. I wonder if Emily knows anything about it."

Prancer ran to the barn door. He jumped up to greet Maddy, licking her cheek.

"Did you buy out the stores?" asked Henry. Maddy giggled from Prancer's sloppy kisses.

"Got a few things." She pulled a small bag from her purse. "Got you toffee bars."

"You stopped at the Sugar-buried Shoppe? I love you!" As soon as he said it, he wondered if he'd embarrassed her, but then he saw a smile break out on her face, even as she turned her head down to conceal it. He grabbed a handful out of the bag.

Kurt said, "Do you two know anything about the cat auditions that are in town?"

"Cat auditions?" Maddy's voice had a lilt as she spoke.

"I heard something about it," said Emily. "Why do you ask?"

"I got a call from a groomer who says she has my renter's cat. Henry says he heard there's an audition going on and putting two and two together, I'm guessing it's her cat."

"If the renter is dead, then who's going to take in her cat?" said Maddy.

Kurt scratched Prancer behind the ears. "I guess it'll go to the shelter."

Maddy shrieked, "No, you can't do that. The poor cat lost its owner and she'll be devastated. It's really hard losing someone you love. Can't we take her in? Please?"

Henry looked at Emily. "It's okay by me."

"Adding a new animal to the mix isn't always easy. Chester is rather set in his ways."

"He'll get used to it," said Maddy. "I'll bet he'll love the company."

Emily couldn't stand to say no. "On one condition. Chester will have to approve."

"I'll send you the address," said Kurt. "Prancer's getting a little impatient for his walk. Let me know what happens. I'd take the cat myself, but you know how the king feels about cats."

After Kurt left, Henry closed up the primer can and followed the girls into the house.

"Can we go pick up the cat now?" asked Maddy. "We have to stop and get food bowls and a litter box, unless you think it can share a litter box with Chester. And what about the commercial? Can we bring the cat to try out? Sounds like he earned his spot."

"First things first," said Emily. Let me check the address and call to make sure they're open." She was hesitant to bring another pet into the household, but it seemed to cheer up Maddy quite a bit—much more than the shopping spree had. "You're coming with us, right, Henry?" the tone of her voice left him without a choice.

"Let me wash off my hands and we're good to go."

The Polished Pet was downtown next to the antiques store. They decided to pick up the cat before the shop closed and worry about the accessories later. A well-dressed couple carrying out a freshly pampered Yorkie squeezed past them on their way in. When they were out of earshot, Henry whispered to Maddy, "Don't you think those pink bows make the dog look idiotic?"

The shop smelled of fresh paint. One of the white, wooden walls was covered by a mural of cats and dogs picnicking by the beach. A chorus of barking came from the back room.

Emily rang the bell on the counter and the owner appeared. "Excuse me. I'm here to pick up Danielle LaPierre's cat."

The owner was a pleasant older woman with strands of gray hair peeking out from under her blue bandana. "Poor kitty's been moping around. He hasn't eaten anything in the past two days. Can't imagine why anyone would leave such a cutie abandoned at my shop. And the owner seemed to care so much about him, too."

Emily said, "I'm sure she loved him very much. Unfortunately, there was a terrible accident and Ms. Pierre is no longer with us."

The owner's hands flew to her mouth. "Oh my God. How awful!"

"Yes, such a tragedy. I'm sure her cat senses it, poor baby." Emily couldn't help thinking of when Fiona died, leaving Maddy behind. "But we're here to make sure her cat has a new home. He'll be well taken care of."

Maddy pet a tabby through its mesh cage while they waited. She and the cat began a two-syllable conversation consisting of 'meow' in varied lengths and pitches.

"Your daughter is a born animal lover. I can always tell."

"She's not really our..." Although Emily was beginning to feel like Maddy's mother, she felt as if she was betraying her deceased friend by taking parental credit.

Henry intercepted. "Yes, Maddy is definitely an animal lover. That's our girl." He saw Maddy roll her eyes at the remark.

"I'll go get Max. He's a real sweetheart."

The owner went into the back. Meanwhile, Henry grabbed a rolling plastic cat toy from the shelf. Emily browsed through a rack of collars, and chose a royal blue one with a safety clasp. Maddy was still occupied with the tabby when the groomer reappeared.

Maddy's eyes lit up like sunshine when she saw the furry, orange cat, Max. Max sniffed her hand and within seconds he was wrapped in her arms, much to the chagrin of the newly abandoned, caged tabby.

"Looks like we have ourselves a second cat," said Henry. He scratched Max behind the ears.

"I'm sure Max's human mother, may she rest in peace, is thrilled to know Max is taken care of." The owner looked toward the door when she heard the familiar jingle announcing a customer. Maddy tightened her hold on her new baby, worried he'd try to jump down, but Max barely reacted. An older woman with a tight, yellowed gray bun entered holding a carrier. Henry thought he recognized her from lunch at Coralee's.

"Hello, are you the owner? I called earlier about having Tiara shampooed before the big audition."

"Yes, I have her slotted in."

"Good. She needs her rest before she makes her acting debut."

Henry said, "Excuse me, but are you here for the national audition?"

"Sure am. Tiara beat out thousands of entrants to make it to the finals. She loves Feline Feast, especially the seafood au gratin. She'll win this hands down."

Emily had nearly forgotten Kurt's comment about 'the big day.' She could see Maddy was all ears. "Excuse me, but when is the competition?"

"Friday, right before Labor Day weekend." She looked at Max in Maddy's arms. "Wait a minute. I know that cat. He was at the semi-finals in D.C. He was with a young lady, older than your daughter."

"Yes, we have Max now," said Emily.

"Did that animal hater boyfriend of hers get her to give him up or something? They were fighting the whole time we were waiting in the green room at the last audition."

"Boyfriend?" said Emily.

"I'm assuming it was her boyfriend. He told her it was the cat or him. He was moving somewhere for his job, I think, and said he couldn't bring a pet. Then she smacked him and told him she chose the cat. Made quite the scene, all that arguing. Tiara was scared out of her mind from the yelling. He was fuming mad. Said she was making a big mistake and stormed out. I'm surprised she wound up giving in and letting the poor kitty go."

Emily said, "You didn't catch his name, did you?"

"She called him Burt, or Bart. Can't remember exactly."

Henry said, "You said the audition took place in the D.C. area? Can you tell us when exactly it was?"

"That I can do." She pulled a notepad from her oversized cat print purse, flipped through her day planner, and jotted down the information. "Take care of the fur baby. I hope I'll see you at the audition."

Henry paid the grooming bill and led the way back to the car.

"There's out first lead," said Emily. "We have to tell the detectives there was an angry boyfriend."

"Not much to go on," said Henry. "Burt or Bart or maybe something else? She's staying at the inn, so the police can easily interview her."

"They can also track down the Feline Feast company. Maybe whoever ran the audition overheard something."

"I doubt it. The audition didn't take place in the green room. Hey, I have another idea. There are two other cat owners staying at Coralee's."

Chapter 5

To Emily's amazement, Max slept on Maddy's lap for the entire car ride. There was no way Chester would have stayed put. He'd have been clawing the seats and trying to jump out a window.

"Chester will have a new friend," said Maddy, as Emily unlocked the front door of their cabin. "Here Chester. We're home."

Chester jumped off the back of the sofa and confronted Max, back arched, tail down.

"I never heard him hiss like that," said Maddy. Max jumped out of her arms, scratching her forearm as he pounced to freedom. Chester ran into the other room.

Emily followed and scooped up her cat. "I'll put Chester in the bedroom."

"What happened?" said Maddy. "My best friend in Chicago had three cats and they all got along."

"They're both spoiled and used to undivided attention. Chester's been an only child for his whole life, and looks like Max got lots of one on one from Danielle. After all, she took the time to travel with him to the auditions and paid a groomer to bathe him. We've never taken Chester to a groomer and we are pretty devoted to him."

Emily returned from the bedroom. "We'll have to introduce them gradually. Maddy, why don't you keep Max in your room for a while after he comes out of hiding, and I'll give him one of Chester's toys so he can get used to his scent. We'll go buy Max a food bowl and his own litter box after dinner."

By the time they sat down to dinner, Max had worked his way out from under the sofa and explored the downstairs. Henry tossed him the rolling cat toy he'd purchased. Emily had thrown together vegetable quesadillas and a salad. Maddy's influence had turned her into a staunch vegetarian.

"If the two cats don't get along, maybe we can convince Kurt to take Max," said Emily. At the mention of Kurt's name, they heard a knock.

"Speak of the devil," said Henry. Kurt stood at the front door with Prancer. "Come on in."

"So what happened with the cat? Did you pick it up?" Prancer growled and tugged at his leash.

"Yes," said Emily, "but if he can't get used to Chester, do you think you can take him?"

"You see how he's reacting already. I told Henry he didn't get along with cats. It would be dangerous. Prancer's a sweetheart, but he hates cats."

"First things first," said Henry. "It may be just fine once he and Chester get used to each other. Turns out Max here was in town for the big cat commercial audition. That's why Danielle LaPierre came here."

Emily added, "We met another contender at the groomers. She said Danielle was fighting with her boyfriend. It could be our first lead."

"Or this can," said Kurt. He pulled a handkerchief from his pocket. "Prancer found this on the ground by the cabin. It smells of smoke. I'll bet it was dropped by the killer."

"Who still uses a handkerchief?" said Maddy.

"No one I know in this community. Unless it's one of the new girls that bought Kiki and Buzz's place. We haven't met them yet," said Emily.

"I'll drop this off for the cops to handle," said Kurt. "Good luck with the new kitty."

After Kurt left, Emily cleared the table and checked her email while Maddy played with Max.

"Henry, look at this email from the new chair. She expects all faculty, even adjunct, to be in attendance all week to prepare for the upcoming semester. She cites some page and paragraph in the faculty code of conduct which, if you ask me, is open to interpretation. Oh my God, she had a time clock installed!"

"I know you enjoy teaching, but if you think working at St. Edwards is going to be more trouble than it's worth, don't do it. We were both supposed to be taking early retirement when we moved up here. And I know, I'm just as guilty. I didn't intend to put in hours at the clinic and the emergency room once we moved, but I felt a calling. I get it."

"I haven't actually met her yet. Maybe she just comes across terribly in emails. Guess I'll find out on Monday. Do you want to do brunch at Coralee's tomorrow?"

"And happen to come across a certain group of cat owners?"

"You got it."

Chester slept by Emily's side all night long. She sincerely hoped he'd come to accept Max. After an uncomfortable night of trying not to move and disturb her cat, Emily woke up stiff and went for an early run. By the time she finished and showered, it was mid-morning.

"I'm hungry, are you ready to go?" asked Henry. He'd been working on the Sunday Sudoku.

"Did you talk to Maddy?"

"She wants to stay home with Max. I told her we'd bring back food."

Emily threw a heavy sweater over her jeans and turtle neck. Her cheeks were still red from her earlier run. To her delight, the morning air hinted at winter, a prelude to the beginning of the school year. In the Jeep, she cracked the passenger side window open and felt the breeze blow through her hair.

When they pulled in front of the Outside Inn, a handful of guests, some wrapped in blankets, rocked in wooden Adirondack chairs, nursing mugs of coffee. An elderly couple sitting around a wooden coffee table worked on the puzzles from the Sunday paper. Coralee, wearing a sweat jacket open over her dress, mingled with her guests. When she saw Emily and Henry, she stepped down off the porch to greet them.

"Where's Maddy?" Her eyes sparkled like blue-gray stars.

"Too worried about our new cat," said Emily. "The murder victim was in town for the cat audition, like you said. To make a long story short, we took in her cat and are hoping he and Chester will be able to coexist."

"Poor thing. Do you think the murder had something to do with the audition? It's very competitive, I hear. Lots of money at stake for the winner."

Henry said, "We were hoping to chat with the other contenders. One of your guests met Danielle in the green room of a previous audition and heard her arguing with a boyfriend."

"So now you're taking the whole cat commercial thing seriously?" Coralee folded her arms across her chest as she spoke.

Henry cleared his throat. "I'm taking *the murder* seriously. One of them may be able to help."

"Come on. I'll find you a table." Before Coralee could hand them the menus, the woman they'd met at the groomers came up behind them.

"Fancy meeting you here! How's Max?"

"Maddy's doting on him. Our own cat isn't too happy."

"You know each other?" said Coralee.

"Sort of," said Emily. "We haven't formally met." She shook the woman's hand. "I'm Emily Fox and this is my husband, Henry."

"Sheila Thompson. Would you like to join us for brunch? The others are already in there."

Not wanting to miss an opportunity to get more information regarding Danielle, Emily agreed. "We'd love to."

Coralee led them through the crowded dining room to a round table in the corner where the others were seated. Half the town's residents came out for Sunday brunch. When the tourists starting showing up to see the foliage, the line went clear out to the porch.

"Tell me you have blueberry French toast this morning," said Henry. "Maddy doesn't know what she's missing."

"Do you want some powdered sugar sprinkled on top?" said Coralee.

Henry glanced at his Fitbit and vowed to take an afternoon walk. "Of course."

Sheila introduced him and Emily to the others.

"This is Winnie Cole, from Oklahoma City." Winnie was younger than Sheila, wore no makeup, and had an edgy look about her.

"You know how they say pets resemble their owners? Look at those green eyes and silky hair. Trudy looks just like Winnie." Sheila sipped her coffee. "And here's our male representative, Pete Gaver." Peter reminded Emily of her grandfather.

"Plenty of guys love cats, you know," he said, "but they won't admit it. Think it's girly. Opt for big dogs instead."

Emily immediately thought of Kurt with his black lab.

"If Pete's cat Floyd wins the audition, just see how many guys change their minds," said Winnie.

Sugary French toast, omelets oozing with ham, and a stack of silver dollar pancakes were brought to the table.

"This is the best French toast I've ever tasted," said Sheila.

"It's my hands down favorite," said Henry. Between bites, he brought up Danielle. "Too bad about the fourth contestant. Our friend was renting his place out to Danielle LaPierre. He found the body."

"How horrible. Danielle was a doll," said Sheila. "I ran into her at three of the auditions and we chatted away. I still can't get over what happened."

"Her parents are away on a cruise. You mentioned a boyfriend."

Sheila put down her fork. "If he was a friend, I'd hate to meet her enemies. Controlling jerk. She was going to leave him after this was all over."

Henry said, "Do you know his name or where he lives?"

"He lived near Danielle in Falls Church. Worked for the government or something. I think he was an engineer. I remember his name now. Brody was what she called him."

"I hate to ask, but do you think their problems were serious enough that he could have killed her?" Henry hoped he wasn't being overtly blunt.

Sheila said, "He sure seemed to have a temper that time they argued back at the D.C. audition. I suppose he could have."

Winnie excused herself from the table. Emily couldn't put her finger on it, but there was something off with Winnie. While the rest of the table truly looked sorry about Danielle's death, Winnie's jaw was firmly set and she didn't chime in with nice comments about Danielle like the others did.

Emily said, "Is Winnie okay?"

"There was no love lost between her and Danielle," said Sheila. "I got the feeling they knew each other before the whole commercial thing started. When Danielle came into a room, Winnie left. And vice versa."

Emily and Henry finished every bite, then headed home to Maddy and the two cats. Full from brunch, they spent most of the afternoon curled up on the sofa watching Netflix. Maddy offered to cook dinner, creating a delicious tofu stir-fry. Emily worried that Maddy suffered from depression and was thrilled to see her energy surge since bringing home Max. Still, an incident with Maddy overdosing on sleeping pills after her mother died nagged at Emily.

She laid out her clothes for the next day and went to bed early, wondering if she should have in fact resigned her new position.

Chapter 6

Beams of morning sun shone through the slats in the kitchen blinds. Henry measured a cup of cornflakes and poured them into a bowl.

"I really wasn't planning on going back to work full time this week," said Emily, "let alone punching a time-clock. Is that insulting or what?" She poured herself a mug of coffee.

"Like I said, you don't have to go," said Henry. "You can stay home and devote yourself to finishing your next book." He was beginning to feel like a broken record.

"If there was a next book. I'm at a loss. The first two went over so well, I'm afraid I won't be able to live up to my reputation. Besides, I have no idea what to write about next."

Henry poured more cereal and said, "It'll come to you just like the last two ideas did. Just be patient. The harder you try, the less likely you are to relax and be inspired."

Maddy, wearing her mother's robe and cuddling Max in her arms, came into the kitchen. "Chester hissed at Max again."

"Give it more time. Why don't you leave your robe where Chester can pick up Max's scent?" Emily glanced at the rooster clock. "I gotta go. All I need is to be late for our first department meeting." She kissed Henry goodbye. She wanted to do the same with Maddy but was sure Maddy would pull away.

On the way to St. Edwards, Emily passed an empty yellow school bus practicing its route for next week. She considered what Henry said. She could stay home and write, maybe learn some new vegetarian recipes. She could even volunteer at Maddy's school. On second thought, she didn't want to smother Maddy. Best to be an achievement-oriented role model like Fiona was. She pulled in front of her three-story building, took a deep breath, and prepared to meet Mair Rose.

Nancy Patterson pulled into the space next to her. "Like the new purse I picked up at the Coach outlet? Half the normal price! Ready for the new semester?" Nancy looked polished in white linen pants with turquoise shoes that matched her blouse. She grabbed an armload of books from the back seat.

"I wasn't ready to plunge in so soon, but yes, I'm looking forward to meeting my new students. I've been working on ideas for my crime writing class all summer."

"That was a great idea. I'm glad our former boss was so supportive."

"I miss Shera already."

They went in the side door of the stone, castle-like building and Nancy followed Emily into her first floor office. Emily sniffed the musty room and cracked open the window.

"This pile of books is killing my arm!"

"Put them down on my desk. I'm glad all my resources are on-line." She looked at her watch. "We have exactly five minutes to get to the meeting."

On the way to the meeting, they stopped in the workroom and punched in with the newly installed time clock.

"Nance, this is utterly humiliating. I didn't even punch a clock when I worked at McDonald's when I was seventeen."

Nancy nodded. "This is going to be a rough year. I feel it already."

When Emily and Nancy walked into the meeting, the other faculty members were already seated in folding chairs. Mair Rose's gritty voice boomed through the stuffy conference room.

"This place is going to run like a well-oiled machine. I've instituted a number of changes which I've emailed to all of you. In your mailboxes, you'll find revised syllabi and a calendar showing data submission deadlines."

Emily whispered to Nancy, "What data?"

Mair glared at the two of them. "As I was saying, get on board or disembark. This ship's sailing with or without you."

Nancy whispered, "Do you see coffee anywhere? Shera always had coffee and pastries at meetings."

Mair said, "The ground rules stated in the email specify professional conduct." She was once again glaring in Nancy and Emily's direction. Her jet black hair was pulled back in a tight ponytail, accentuating her pasty, freckled skin. Her clothes were two sizes too small.

"How about professional dress?" whispered Emily. "The button across her chest is about to pop."

After reading off a ten slide power point, the new chair finally said, "Meeting adjourned. Clock out for lunch. Thirty minutes max." She strutted out of the room balanced on three inch heels.

After comparing notes with the others in the room, the forecast indicated a stormy, miserable year. Emily's plan was to avoid her new boss as much as possible, knowing she could quit if it got too bad. At least she was still excited about the new crime writing class she'd be teaching. She and Nancy stopped at their mailboxes. Emily pulled out a stack of papers and flipped through them.

"What! She's got to be kidding," said Emily. "This revised syllabus isn't the course I was supposed to teach. It's basic writing, not crime writing." Her stomach dropped to her feet.

Nancy looked over her shoulder. "It's more basic than what you taught last year. I'm not happy either. Look at the red marks all over what I submitted."

Emily went back to her office and tried to busy herself organizing her things. She didn't know where Mair was coming from but she wasn't anxious to be in her crosshairs.

*****

Henry left for the hospital shortly after Emily went to the campus. He treated a sprained ankle and prescribed antibiotics for a toddler's ear infection, then found himself with a little down time. He took the elevator to the morgue, where he found Pat typing up notes.

"Hey, buddy. If you're looking for new patients I'm afraid you're too late."

"Speaking of too late, didn't you have time to change your clothes this morning? Looks like you slept in that wrinkled shirt," said Henry.

"Maybe I had a better way to spend my time."

"So things are ramping up between you and Megan? I'm happy for you."

Pat responded, "It's the best I've felt in all the years since my wife died."

"Treat her right. Don't go doing anything to screw it up."

"Yeah, yeah. By the way, I thought you'd like to know that Megan says the victim's boyfriend is flying into town later today. Her parents are still away."

"From what one of the cat ladies said, their relationship was volatile," said Henry. "I wouldn't be surprised if he snapped and killed her."

"Carbon monoxide poisoning isn't the kind of thing you snap and do, like stabbing or strangling someone," said Pat. "It takes careful planning, and prior access to where she lived. The fireplace was blocked, and the plastic foam you found was used to seal the door and windows to make sure the gas would be lethal. It doesn't ring of a lover's spat to me."

"True, but we haven't met the guy yet. Nor do we know how long they were having problems. Got anything better to go on?"

Pat's phone rang. "Yeah, send him down."

"More business?"

"Yeah. We'll catch up later."

Henry checked in at the ER, which was surprisingly quiet. He read a few images that were sitting on his desk and wrote out his findings. By the time he finished, another patient was waiting to see him. He recognized her from brunch.

The woman was scratching her arms. "You're the man I met at the inn yesterday. I didn't know you were a doctor."

"That's me, Dr. Fox. You're Winnie Cole from Oklahoma, right? The nurse says you're having an allergic reaction." He could see red welts on Winnie's arms and face.

"I must have come in contact with a synthetic fabric. I think it was the bedspread. I can only wear cotton; my skin is hyper sensitive."

"Are you having any respiratory symptoms?"

"My throat feels tight and I'm itching like crazy. Doc back home gives me an antihistamine and prednisone. Sometimes a cream too."

"How do you manage to have a cat? If people are allergic to anything it's usually cats...or peanuts."

"Never had a problem with animals. Just gotta watch what I touch. If I so much as wipe my face with a colored paper napkin my skin goes crazy."

Henry wrote out a prescription. "Have you lived out in Oklahoma all your life? Seasonal allergies aren't so bad out there."

"I moved there a few years back. Used to live right outside of our capital. Got a better paying job offer so I packed up my cat and off we went. I like it. Less hectic than the city."

Henry ripped the script from the pad and handed it to her. "This should help. Call me if it isn't better in a few hours."

The rest of the day was quiet and by late afternoon he was home. Emily stormed in the front door right after him.

"I can't believe this woman! She nixed the course I've been working on all summer and she's a tyrant. We have a time clock. A time clock! Like factory workers or the people who man the toll booths. Since when is department chair a power position anyway? Shera never treated us like underlings. She was there to help us and always wanted our input."

"Where this lady come from?"

"I don't know. I think she said Camden College."

Henry grabbed his laptop. "How do you spell her name?" He googled Camden College while waiting for Emily's response. "She isn't on their roster from last year."

Maddy ran into the living room, chasing Max who'd escaped from her room. Chester was waiting at the entrance to the kitchen and swatted at Max.

"Maddy, I don't think this is going to work out," said Emily.

"I don't want Chester to be miserable, but we can't drop Max off at the shelter," moaned Maddy.

"I have an idea," said Henry. "Coralee has space at the inn. Maybe she'll take him. Her cat died last winter and she was heartbroken."

"Let's give it another day, okay? If they still hate each other we can ask Coralee," begged Maddy.

Emily agreed, proud of Maddy for being willing to let Max go to a better suited home.

Chapter 7

Emily punched the time clock at exactly 9:01 the next morning, her protest within acceptable limits. What she didn't find acceptable was having to rewrite, no, *trash* the course she'd worked so hard putting together.

She looked through the new syllabus and thought elementary students would have difficulty finding it challenging, let alone undergrads. True, it was going to be an elective, but the students who registered for it were expecting a course in crime writing. Now she was working on a dry, intro course which touched upon half a dozen types of writing, never getting deeply into any one of them. Her mind kept drifting and her eyes checked the clock at regular intervals.

"Knock, knock," said Nancy. "Surviving?" She carried two coffees from the newly opened Starbuck's near the campus.

"My heart just isn't into teaching this course. I have other things on my mind."

"How's Maddy doing with school starting next week? Brooke says she's tried to text her but Maddy doesn't answer."

"Maddy's preoccupied with Max the cat at the moment. Looks like we will have to find him a new home since Chester doesn't want any part of sharing. Do you think Brooke…"

"No way. She and I are both allergic. Max. That's the cat that belonged to the murder victim, right? Have you heard anything more about the investigation?"

"Nada. The boyfriend was supposed to have flown in yesterday but I haven't heard anything. Only…"

"Only what?"

"It's far-fetched, but one of the other cat owners here for the commercial audition lived in the same town as Danielle and her boyfriend. Henry was talking to her. She's out in Oklahoma now, but she acted strange when we were at the inn the other day. I can't put my finger on it."

"You could google her. See if you find any common threads."

"There must be a million Winnie Coles."

"She belongs to some cat club no doubt. Start there."

Emily had barely starting typing when Mair Rose appeared at the door. Her black hair fell over her bare shoulders. Even if it was the style, having shoulder holes cut into your blouse looked unprofessional.

"Good. You're both here." She pulled two lists off of her clipboard. "These are the committees I put you on, as well as your advising hours and office hours. Committees meet every Wednesday at 8 a.m. Remember, professional collaboration is part of your formal evaluations."

Emily listened to Mair's heels clicking like daggers into the linoleum all the way down the hallway. She closed her office door with a slam.

"Since when do we have formal evaluations?" said Emily.

"Emily, why are you staying? I'd miss you terribly, but if I didn't need the money, no way would I put up with this hostile work environment."

"I've been entertaining the idea. I don't want Maddy to see me as a quitter, or as someone who spends her days in her pajamas. Also, I'm going to sock every paycheck into a college fund for her. Fiona was a single

Mom and didn't leave much of anything for Maddy's future."

"Noble, but I'd keep my options open. Better get back to work."

Emily half worked, half daydreamed until she could officially leave campus. On her way home, Henry texted her. He had Maddy with him and they were heading to the inn for dinner with Pat and Megan. He asked her to meet them there.

When she arrived, she spotted Pat, his detective girlfriend, and *her family* at a round table near the French doors. Megan looked cute in a jumpsuit that complimented her strawberry-colored hair. Pat looked happier than she'd ever seen him. His eyes twinkled whenever he looked at Megan.

Henry stood up and held Emily's chair. "Hey, glad you made it. Didn't think you'd feel like cooking after a day at the prison."

"You got that right! Megan, how are you? Pat told us you were renovating your cabin."

"It's more work than I'd anticipated. I'm having to hire help. In fact, Noah is changing the carpet and putting in recessed lighting for me. Coralee trained him well. Franklin will be taking over once Noah starts back at school."

Emily whispered to Maddy, "Franklin is Coralee's handyman."

Pat said, "Megan got to interview the victim's boyfriend yesterday. He's an engineer. Works in D.C."

"How did he seem?" said Emily.

Megan put down her iced tea. "He acted upset, but he's hiding something. Said he hadn't seen Danielle since the previous audition, the one where he made a huge scene in the green room."

"He's an engineer," said Henry. "He knows how to rig up carbon monoxide."

Megan said, "The only clues we have are the handkerchief which smells like smoke, the empty cigarette pack, and the clothing stuffed into the chimney. Can't tie any of those to him. He's not a smoker, definitely too young to use a handkerchief, and the clothes in the chimney…a plaid jacket several sizes larger than he wears, and an old beret."

Maddy, usually shy in social situations, said, "Check the thrift shop. He could have run in and bought those items to stuff the chimney with. If he's smart enough to be an engineer, he wouldn't leave behind his own clothing."

Henry admired how Maddy always seemed to see things through practical eyes. He imagined if he'd had a biological daughter she'd have been a lot like her.

Pat said, "That's true, but what about the cigarettes?"

"Anyone could have dropped the cigarette pack or the handkerchief. They don't necessarily belong to the killer," said Emily.

"And the foam weather stripping? Don't forget that," added Pat. "Megan, are you going to check the hardware store?"

"I've got it covered. Now, let's order. I'm starving."

Chapter 8

The next morning, Emily went for a run before work. Maddy had bonded with Max immediately. How would she handle leaving him behind at the inn? She was preoccupied the entire day, getting little done in her office. When she arrived home, Maddy was brushing Max and speaking softly to him. She rubbed her cheek against his fur.

"He loves being brushed, doesn't he?" said Emily.

"He's been purring the whole time. We're still bringing him to the audition on Friday, right?"

"Of course. Are you doing okay, Maddy?"

"Coralee really misses her cat and I'm sure Max will be happy at the inn. I wish he could stay with us, but Chester is miserable and he was here first."

"We eat at the inn at least once a week," said Emily. "And you can ride your bike over any time you want to see him."

"I know. I'm okay with it. Sometimes you have to do what's best for someone you love even if it isn't best for you."

Henry came in from the garage. "Hey, I painted the bookshelf. Tomorrow I'll give it a second coat, and you'll have it in your room before school starts."

"Thanks, Henry."

Maddy packed up Max's things and carried him out to the car. She held him tight the whole ride over to the inn. As soon as Max saw Coralee, he rubbed against her legs. Coralee's face softened into a wide smile as she bent down to pet him.

"I've missed Jacky so much since he died. I couldn't bring myself to adopt another cat until Max came along. I feel like it was meant to be."

Henry said, "But remember, if he wins that commercial audition and snags a contract, we get the money. You can have the free cat food."

Winnie, wearing boots and a jacket, and Sheila, dressed in heavy layers, came in from outside. It had been getting cooler, but Emily thought they must be sweating under all that. After all, she hadn't even taken out all her fall sweaters yet.

Coralee said, "How was your walk?"

"Great. This is a quaint little town if I ever saw one." Sheila bent down to pet Max. "Max? What are you doing here, baby?"

"He's my new pet and official mascot of the Outside Inn." Coralee beamed like a proud parent.

Winnie bent down beside Sheila to pet Max. "Hey, big guy. I'm so sorry about your mommy." She rubbed her face against his fur. "Oh my goodness, we're tangled!"

Emily bent down. "He's got his paw stuck in your necklace. Here, I've got it."

She and Winnie stood up. "What a beautiful locket. It looks like an antique."

"It was my Mom's. It's all I have left of her."

"I'm sorry," said Emily.

"It's been a few years, but I still haven't gotten over it. Senseless death. She had another decade in her at least. Someday they'll pay for what happened. It's not over yet."

Emily was puzzled by the comment, but before she could ask questions, a broad shouldered gentleman carrying an overnight bag walked up to the desk.

"Excuse me. I need a room and I was directed here."

Coralee kissed the top of Max's head and wiped her hands on her apron. "Certainly. Welcome to the Outside Inn, Mr…"

"Wilkerson. Brody Wilkerson."

Both Emily and Henry whipped their heads around. Emily mouthed 'that's him' to Henry. Brody waited while Coralee took his credit card and handed him a key. Winnie stood up with a huff and stared at him.

"Do I know you or something?" said Brody.

Winnie shook her head and marched back to her room. Emily was baffled by Winnie's confusing behavior. If they had ever run into each other, it would only have been at a prior audition. It didn't surprise her that Brody may not have remembered meeting her.

Sheila said, "That's Danielle's boyfriend. He's the one who made the scene back in D.C. Do you think he came to identify the body?"

"Maybe," said Emily. "Was Winnie there when he fought with Danielle?"

"I didn't see her, but we were all scheduled for different times so she may have been. Why?"

"It's nothing." She glanced at her watch. "We'd better be getting home," said Emily. She studied Maddy's expression, worried there'd be tears.

Maddy gave the cat one more kiss before following Henry and Emily out to the car. She turned to Emily. "Don't look so worried. I'm really okay with this. It's not like Max died or anything. I'll still see him." She crawled into the back seat.

On the way home, Pat called.

"Hey, just wanted to follow up after last night. Megan and her partner Ron went over to the hardware store this afternoon. They sell the type of weather sealant you found, but the owner says the only person who purchased it in the past few months was Coralee's handyman, Franklin."

"I'm assuming he needed it for the inn."

"That's what he said. Coralee confirmed he was making some repairs and sealing cracks around the windows for her."

"Did the detectives check out the thrift shop?"

"Yeah. No one's bought any clothing from them in a while. Books and bric-a-brac, yes; clothing, no."

"Thanks for letting us know. You're still coming by for the cookout on Labor Day, right?"

"I'll bring the beer. Oops, is Maddy in the car with you? I forget how the phone broadcasts itself through the car on that fancy-schmanzy Jeep of yours."

Maddy groaned in the back seat.

"I'll bring *the drinks*. See ya at the hospital, buddy."

When they got home, Emily pulled chopped vegetables from the fridge. Henry poured oil into the Wok and sliced the tofu. If anyone had told him he'd be eating tofu several nights a week before they took in Maddy, he would have said they were crazy.

"I never asked how your day went," said Henry.

"I can't stand Mair Rose," said Emily. "She's the most abrasive person I've ever had to work with, and that includes the eager-for-a-story reporters at the paper. There's a difference between being aggressive to get a job done and being just plain nasty." She threw the vegetables into the Wok and called, "Maddy, can you set the table?"

Minutes later Maddy came in carrying Chester.

"Wash your hands," said Emily.

"I know. I'm not stupid." She grumbled as she put out the silverware.

"My friend Nancy says her daughter has been trying to get in touch with you but you never respond."

"Am I obligated to respond?"

"Of course not, but..."

"Then mind your own business and let me handle my social life."

Henry said, "You can't talk to Emily like that. Apologize."

"Sorry. I hate when she acts like she's my mother. She's nothing like my mother."

Emily held back tears and they ate in silence.

Maddy took a few bites, pushed the food around on her plate, then said, "May I be excused?"

"Go," said Henry. "And stay in your room until you have a better attitude." She mimicked him under her breath as she stomped away from the table.

Emily refused to let herself cry. She was the adult and Maddy's brain wouldn't be fully formed for another ten years. Besides, this was normal. She'd read it in *Parents' Magazine*. Teenagers rebel in order to solidify their independence.

"She didn't mean it," said Henry.

"I know. She had a hard day turning Max over and everything." She wished she felt that casual over Maddy's words, but the truth was she felt like a deflated balloon. "You know, I was thinking, remember how we talked about adopting Maddy?"

"Yes, and you thought it was too soon."

"I know, but I'm beginning to think it's not such a bad idea." Of all moments, she wasn't sure why she felt compelled to revisit adoption at just this point in time.

"It would give her a sense of stability, I suppose." He began clearing the table. "And then she'd have to listen to us. Kids listen to their parents, right?" He winked at her.

"Sure they do." She lingered on the word *sure*. "Maybe after she gets past the start of the school year we can discuss it with her."

"Sounds like a plan."

Chapter 9

Friday came quickly. Maddy and Emily spent the week researching pet auditions and Maddy had spent time at Coralee's every day after school preparing Max for the big day. She'd been up since dawn brushing Max until she could see herself in his shiny coat.

"Maddy, I made scrambled eggs. Come and eat something."

"I'm too nervous. Should I bring food for Max? I packed his water bowl, his brush, and his favorite toy."

"Sure. Put some in a sandwich bag." While Emily tossed the box to Maddy, she grabbed a handful of chewy granola bars from the pantry in case Maddy got hungry later.

Emily parked in front of the three-story office building and helped Maddy get Max out of the car. The modern glass building looked out of place nestled between an old fashioned book store and an artsy boutique which hadn't yet opened for the day. Emily watched Maddy twist a strand of hair around her finger and knew she was nervous about the audition. They walked past a law office and a mortgage office into a conference room where Sheila, Winnie, and Pete sat waiting with their cats.

"Good morning," said Sheila. Her teal pantsuit and matching headband brought out her eyes. "Is Max ready? They will be starting any minute."

Emily looked at Max who was asleep in his carrier. "Ready as ever."

Pete Gaver stood up. "Well, good morning. Who's this pretty little lady? I met your mom at the inn but I didn't meet you. Pete Gaver." He extended his hand to Maddy. "Max doesn't get phased by this Hollywood stuff. Danielle had to coax him out of the cage for the semi-finals. He doesn't like having his naps interrupted."

Maddy peeked in the carrier next to Pete's chair. "What's his name?"

"Floyd, like on *Green Acres*."

Maddy said, "Huh?"

"The TV show. Never mind. You're way too young to have seen it."

A young man carrying a clipboard opened the door. "Are we ready? First up we need Tiara."

Sheila said, "Wish us luck," and followed the young man down the hall.

"I wonder if they'll let us know who wins today." said Maddy.

Winnie said, "I hope so. I have a flight out this afternoon. Whoever wins I'm sure will have to go to their headquarters and look through the contract. I'm anxious to get home. Today would have been my Mom's ninetieth birthday and I told my sister I'd spend the evening with her."

"I'm so sorry," said Emily.

"The three of us were very close and my sister took her death even harder than I did. After she spent all that money on the case and then we lost! Neither of us has recovered, but she wound up having to sell her house."

Emily could relate to the sister bond. "That's terrible. What case was that?" Emily's reporter instincts kicked in.

"Mom died from heat exhaustion when the air conditioning went out at her assisted living residence. Three days and the place kept it secret while they tried to get it repaired. She wasn't the only one who died either."

"I'm sure you miss her a lot."

"Only good that came out of it was my sister moved to Oklahoma and lives down the street. Cost of living is much cheaper there than it was in D.C. And I found a great job."

"What's your cat's name?" asked Maddy.

"Gertrude. I named her after my mother." A tear appeared on her cheek and she dabbed it with a handkerchief she pulled out of her purse.

Pete flipped through a magazine; Maddy scrolled through her phone. Emily was surprised by her own anxiety. After all, she wasn't the one auditioning. She knew Maddy would be disappointed if Max wasn't picked, but if he did win, their schedules would be thrown into a tailspin with school starting. Would Mair Rose outright fire her if she needed time off to take the cat to his obligations?

The man with the clipboard reappeared. "Next up is Gertrude."

Winnie said, "Best of luck to all. May the best cat win."

Emily sat down next to Pete. "Do you know the case she was talking about?"

"I don't get too caught up in the chit chat, but I heard her tell Sheila something about a lawsuit involving a nursing home. Some sort of negligence."

Emily pulled out her Kindle and savored the time to catch up on her reading. Maddy gave Max a pep talk, then took him out and brushed him once again till he shined. Finally, it was Max's turn. They followed the young man into a conference room where two women sat behind a table with a Feline Feast banner draped over it. A makeshift living room was set up at one end of the room. An older gentleman gave the instructions.

"I'll open the can of food, and you let the cat out of his carrier. We have trainers to work with whoever wins the part. For today, we want to see how he does around people and how he responds to directions."

He opened the food and Maddy opened the cage. Max sauntered out and immediately went for the food. The man dangled a cat toy and watched Max bat at it. Then, he wound up a noisy, animated mouse. Emily supposed they wanted to know if Max was easily spooked. She knew Chester would have run for the hills the moment he was let out of confinement. Max handled it like a pro.

"He's a handsome fella. Good temperament, too. We'll be making a decision after we've seen all the finalists. Is this the correct phone number?" He showed her what he had written on the clipboard.

Emily scanned the page trying to read the notes he'd made. 'trainable, good presence...'

"Is it correct?" The man clutched the clipboard to his chest.

"Yes, that's it."

"Thank you for bringing him by."

In the car, Maddy couldn't stop talking about how great Max had done. Emily shared the comments she read, giving both hope that just maybe Max would become a star. They stopped at the inn to drop off Max and eat a late lunch. Coralee ran to them.

"How'd it go? Did they love our boy?"

Maddy said, "He was great. Calmly ate the food, played, wasn't spooked by a noisy toy."

"Let's just say we were proud of him," said Emily.

Winnie, carrying a suitcase and colorful cat carrier, spotted them. "How'd Max do?"

Maddy said, "He did great. How about Gertrude?"

"She was a little wound up. She ran away when the noisy mouse started across the room. I doubt she'll be picked for this one, but we started working with a trainer back home so there will be other chances."

Maddy rubbed her hand over a felt applique on the cat's carrier. "Where'd you get the cool sticker?"

"At the stationery store downtown. There's a big crack underneath it which I couldn't glue together so this was Plan B."

Brody came out of the dining room. "Coralee, can I get some extra towels?"

"Sure. Wait right here and I'll get them."

Winnie's expression hardened and she shifted her weight back and forth. Emily felt Winnie was restraining herself from saying something to Brody, for whatever reason. Brody didn't seem to notice.

"I've got a plane to catch," said Winnie. "Tell Coralee goodbye for me. And good luck. Maybe I'll see Max's face on a can of Feline Feast one day."

When Maddy and Emily went into the dining room, they spotted Sheila sipping a cup of coffee.

"Well, how'd Max do?" asked Sheila.

"I was proud of him," said Emily. "How about Tiara?"

"Also proud. She snuggled right up to the guy with the clipboard when he was verifying our information. She's used to auditions. I've been bringing her to them since she was a kitten. She's registered with an agency and every now and then they call us. She got a photo shoot for a catalog last year."

"That's super," said Emily. She wondered if she should search for such an agency. If there was one at all, the nearest would probably be in Burlington.

"Have a seat. Were you the last to go?"

"Pete was after us. We are starving; did you eat?"

"Ate and polished off dessert too but I'll sit with you and finish my coffee. Tiara's sleeping on the bed."

Maddy and Emily ordered veggie paninis.

"Sheila, Pete said he heard you and Winnie talking about a law suit she was involved in."

"Yes, it involved her mother. Remember the heat spell back a few years ago? The whole eastern coast had record temperatures."

"I do remember. We were living in Westbrook, New York, back then with no air-conditioning!"

"Her mother was in an assisted living facility and the AC stopped working. Brand new building. Anyhow, she died of heatstroke along with a handful of other residents. The nursing home blamed the air conditioning company. The company swore they'd followed code and in turn blamed the owners of the facility for overloading the circuits. It was all over the news."

"Now I remember. Our newspaper covered it. I take it Winnie lost."

"It gets worse. The home required all assets to be signed over to the facility before the patient entered to insure payment."

"Never heard of such a thing."

"It's not as bad as it sounds. If and when the resident runs out of funds, the company still keeps them on for life. It's like having insurance against outliving your savings."

"So how does that relate to Winnie's mother?"

"Winnie and her sister lost their inheritance. All their family money now belonged to the facility and after losing the law suit, Winnie and her sister were out of luck. The facility even kept the jewelry and rare coins Winnie's mother kept in her room. Those items had sentimental value and were supposed to be passed on to the girls. I feel so bad for Winnie."

Coralee brought the paninis to the table.

"I'll leave you girls to eat. I'm going to go join Tiara for a nap. It feels like midnight. Such an exciting morning."

Emily bit into the panini, melted cheese oozing out from the toast. She wondered why Winnie had an issue with Brody. Then again, isn't Falls Church close to D.C? Was it possible they'd met before?

Chapter 10

Emily and Maddy fell asleep early, exhausted from the day's excitement. They woke to a beautiful day for a barbeque—warm but not summery hot. After breakfast, they straightened up the house while Henry mowed the lawn and cleaned the grill. Megan and Pat arrived at noon.

Henry flipped over the veggie burgers, promising he would cook them before actual meat touched the rack. Emily carried out a bowl of potato salad. A small slab of concrete served as the backyard patio, and Maddy, Pat, and Megan sat at the same homemade picnic table Henry's father had made so many years ago.

"So are we going to see Max on TV anytime soon?" asked Pat.

"No," said Maddy. "He did a great job, but he lost to a cat named Tiara."

"I'm sorry to hear that. You must be disappointed."

"It's okay. Tiara is a veteran in the business. We aren't at all sure how much or if Max ever even worked with a trainer."

Megan, hair pulled back in a red, white, and blue bow, said, "I hear they hardly make any money doing those commercials. And it must be stressful for the owner as well as the cat."

"Max seems perfectly happy living at the inn with Coralee," said Henry. "I don't think he's upset about losing."

Emily passed out paper plates. "Maddy and I both start classes tomorrow. We're going to have our hands full. Can you believe Maddy is starting high school?" She felt awkward saying that. After all, it's not like she was there when Maddy started kindergarten or middle school. Then again, she *would* be at her high school graduation, and college, and when she graduated medical school...no, veterinary school would be more likely. She and Henry would be beside Maddy for all the important milestones from now on.

"Who likes their burgers rare?" called Henry. When no one responded, he tried again. "Medium...going once, going twice..." Both Pat and Megan raised their hands like school kids.

Henry brought over the burgers. "So what's Detective Ron doing today?"

"He's with his parents," said Megan. "He's going to meet his new nephew for the first time. He's been showing pictures all week down at the station. The baby looks just like his sister."

"Megan, what ever happened with Danielle's boyfriend? Is he still in town?" asked Emily.

"He says last time he saw her was at the D.C. audition. They had a big fight, and as far as he knew, they were over as a couple. Says Danielle didn't return any of his calls and he figured it was time to move on. We have nothing tying him to the murder."

"Did he have an alibi?"

"Says he was home alone. We have no reason to doubt him. We checked his credit card records—no plane tickets or hotel stays. His boss said he was on a conference call with him the afternoon after Danielle was killed."

"There was this woman, Winnie Cole, at the audition," said Emily. "She acted strange when she saw him. I think they lived near each other at one time. She's in Oklahoma now. Seemed like there was a history there."

"Like they were once a couple?"

"She's quite a bit older than him. I don't think it was that. Just a gut feeling."

"Speaking of guts," said Henry. "I'm still hungry. Maddy made brownies for dessert."

Maddy went inside to retrieve the brownies. Megan grabbed the ice cream they'd bought. Inside the kitchen, Megan asked, "Are you excited about starting school?"

"Not really. I don't know anybody here."

"I know it's hard. My parents moved right when I was starting high school. I hated them for it, but by Christmas I had some friends that I clicked with. You like animals. The school has an excellent 4-H program, and I know some of the local kids have horses. It'll be okay. If you need anything, let me know. Anybody gives you trouble, tell them you have a detective looking out for you."

Megan grabbed the ice cream and followed Maddy back outside.

"Max!" shouted Maddy. Coralee and her son Noah walked into the yard.

Coralee, wearing a flag-colored skort with white tennis shoes said, "I wanted to drop by and tell you how much the guests are loving having Max around. And he revels in the company. When he started going into the dining area I said 'no' and clapped my hands loudly. Guess what? He turned around. I tried it every time he went near. That cat knows the word no."

Emily said, "That's wonderful. I'll bet Danielle trained him or had a professional do it. Sheila said most cats doing the commercial circuit are professionally trained."

"Anyhow, the guests just love him. Maddy, I wanted to thank you again for trusting me to take him."

"I'm glad he's happy. Chester sure is happier."

"Noah's working on building him a cat tree. We'll paint it to look like a real tree and put it in the corner of the lobby."

Noah said, "Franklin had some leftover supplies. I'm even cushioning the branches. You'll have to come see it."

Kurt Olav walked into the yard with Prancer.

"Glad you made it, buddy," said Henry. "You're just in time for dessert."

Henry dished out the ice cream and Maddy passed around the brownies. After barking at Max became boring, Prancer settled down on the lawn and closed his eyes.

"Detective, I was going to drop by the station tomorrow but you saved me the trip. I was cutting the low branches at the cabin—you know the ones that fall against the roof when the snow gets heavy in the winter. It's probably nothing."

Detective Megan said, "The most insignificant observations in my experience have cracked cases."

"I pulled the ladder out of the shed and the bottom rung had dried mud on it, like someone used it to rub the mud off this shoe. On the next step you can see an impression if you look hard. More like a boot than a shoe I'd say. I haven't used that ladder since last winter and it was right after a snowstorm I'm sure I didn't have mud on my shoes."

"You didn't try to clean it, did you?"

"Naw, I knew better. Thought it might be something you could use."

Megan said, "Detective Ron and I assumed the murderer used the wood pile next to the housetop to get to the roof, but we could be wrong. We'll check it out first thing in the morning."

Emily said, "Winnie lives in Oklahoma, and she was wearing cowboy boots the other day."

Henry said, "I saw her at the emergency room. She's in good shape for her age. I'll bet she'd have been able to climb up to the roof without much problem."

"And Brody is young and fit. If he snuck in..."

"Megan said he wasn't in town," said Pat.

"No," said Emily, "she said they didn't find a plane ticket or credit card receipts. There's more than one way to travel."

Storm clouds had moved in and a clap of thunder brought Prancer to his feet. Rain fell from the sky and everyone grabbed what they could carry, running into the house before the storm.

Chapter 11

"Are you ready for your first day of school?" asked Henry. Anxious over Maddy's first day, he hadn't slept well, and got up early to make whole wheat pancakes. Back in high school, he had been bullied and he worried that being an outsider, Maddy could be a target. When he looked at Maddy, she seemed so vulnerable. She'd been moping around the cabin for a week and last night he peeked in to find her crying and hugging her mother's picture.

"I'm not hungry," said Maddy. Chester jumped up on her lap as if to comfort her.

"You'll be hungry later. Your lunch might not be until late." Henry plopped a plate of pancakes in front of her. "It took me hours, you know. First I had to pick the wheat, then grind it, and squish almonds for the milk since we all know how horrible dairy is for us."

Maddy smiled and took a bite. "Stop worrying. I'll be okay."

Emily, hair still wet from her shower, grabbed a cup of coffee.

"How was your run? Any dead bodies?" Henry still teased her after she'd found a corpse on one of her runs the previous summer.

"Good. I can feel it getting cooler in the mornings and I'm ready to ditch the humidity." She speared a few pancakes. "Maddy, you look pretty. Aren't those the jeans we got at the outlet mall?"

"Yeah."

"Did you talk to Brooke? Nancy said she would show you around and introduce you to some new friends."

"I don't need to have my hand held. I'm not starting kindergarten."

Had she not just finished a run, she'd have been on edge enough to spit back something like 'then act like it' or 'lose the chip on your shoulder.' Instead, she took a deep breath and ate her pancakes, repeating her mantra inside her head: *this is what teenagers do…their brains aren't fully formed…*

"Can I walk you to the bus stop?" said Henry. "I'll give you a big hug and kiss goodbye in front of your new classmates. That's okay, right?"

"Ugh," said Maddy. "I'm going to finish getting ready."

"You're so natural with her," said Emily. "I wish I could relax more and stop worrying if everything I say or do is the right thing."

"I had a lot of cousins growing up. Be yourself. She isn't going to break." He wished he fully believed that.

Maddy reappeared. "I'm going now. See you later."

Emily said, "Do you have your notebook and a pen and…"

Henry interrupted. "Your lunch is on the counter. Knock 'em dead."

Maddy bent down to kiss Chester, then closed the door behind her. Emily wished she could run after Maddy and shadow her all day long to be sure she was safe. She wondered how it would have felt if Maddy was going off to preschool or kindergarten for the first time. If it was this scary letting go of a teenager, how did parents manage letting go of their little babies?

You won't be embarrassed if I kiss *you* goodbye, right?" said Henry to Emily.

She grabbed him and said, "I'd be mad if you didn't."

After Emily left, Henry called the hospital to see if he was needed. The ER was quiet with the town focused on the first day of school, giving him a few hours at home to himself. He'd finished the bookshelf for Maddy and hadn't yet started a new project. He grabbed his laptop and did some research. The story Emily had told him about Winnie's mother and the nursing home sounded familiar. After a short while, he'd found what he was looking for.

Nature's Vista assisted living facility in Falls Church was opened the year before the record heat wave. It received much publicity for being state of the art— energized with a newly patented hydro-solar cooling system, *Splash Panels*. The new system promised to be allergy free (the heated water washed away dust before it could accumulate in the duct work), environmentally friendly, and cost efficient.

Henry's phone vibrated. "Hey, Pat. Did things pick up at the hospital?"

"Quiet as a morgue down here. What are you up to?"

"Putzing around on the computer. Pat, do you remember hearing about a nursing home in Virginia back a few years ago that was in the headlines during the Great Eastern Heat Wave?"

"Sounds familiar."

"Ten residents died when the air conditioning unit gave out. The place didn't report it or transport the overheated residents, because they were concerned about the risks of moving them, or so they claimed. Word was it had more to do with the financial implications."

"Oh yeah. My broker mentioned it. Said the stock was going to shoot way up once Splash Panels proved itself. After the deaths, the stock hit rock bottom.

Wasn't there some tie in between the company and the nursing home, like the same owner?"

"Let's find out." Henry took a few minutes to search.

"Splash Panels. Clean, energy efficient…I remember the ads on TV. Find anything?"

"Here we go. Nope, not the same owner. At least, I can't find the owner's name."

Pat's phone buzzed. "I've got to go—just got a new 'patient.' Maybe we can get together and watch the game this weekend."

"I'll bring the beer and pretzels." Henry loved a challenge and set out to find the connection between the nursing home, Splash Panels, and the deaths at the facility. Did the nursing home sue Splash Panels? Nature Vista bought a service and the company failed to provide that service. The nursing home should have sided with the patients against the AC company. He heard the key in the door.

"Emily? You're home early."

"I only teach one class on Tuesday, and the dragon lady went out of town for the holiday. What are you up to?"

"The hospital didn't need me so I've been doing some research. You said Winnie Cole's mother died in an assisted living facility. I found an article about ten deaths due to the Great Eastern Heat Wave at a place called Nature's Vista in Falls Church. They were the first establishment to use Splash Panels—a newly patented air cooling system. When the system gave out, and ten people died, families of the affected patients filed a law suit against the facility and against Splash Panels."

"And the families lost against both. I remember the case. But how does that relate to Danielle's murder? She didn't kill Winnie's mother."

"No, but I did some more digging. Danielle LaPierre was a lawyer, right? Guess who defended Splash Panels?" said Henry.

"No way!"

Henry continued. "Winnie ran into Danielle at a previous audition and realized Danielle was the defense lawyer, I'm guessing. Winnie lost her job and had a nervous breakdown after the trial."

"So you're saying she plotted to kill Danielle when they went to the Vermont Finals. I saw Winnie use a handkerchief at Coralee's! I didn't connect the dots at the time, but Kurt's dog Prancer found a handkerchief near the crime scene. I'll bet it's hers."

"You're jumping a few pieces," said Henry. "The police will have to prove the handkerchief was Winnie's first. That may not be easy."

"What about DNA?"

"Not as quick or simple as they make it out to be on TV."

"Winnie was wearing cowboy boots when I ran into her at the inn. She's living out in Oklahoma so it makes sense she'd have them. I'll bet it was her boot print on the ladder."

"I'll call the detectives and tell them what we learned. Do you hear the bus?" He and Emily ran to the front door and held it open. Emily's heart raced and she squeezed Henry's hand.

"How was school?" shouted Emily, as soon as she was in ear shot.

Maddy slumped by them. She threw her backpack on the sofa and headed toward her room. Emily and Henry followed her.

"Hey, did you have a bad day?" said Emily. Trite as it was, the unedited sentiment flew out of her mouth.

"Bad? Try horrible. Try the worst day in my life since my Mom died."

Henry put his arm around her. Surprisingly, she didn't pull away. "What happened?"

"The kids all know each other. I'm the outsider. The only one who recognized my existence was Brooke."

"Did you eat lunch with her?" asked Emily.

"She was with her friends. She asked, but I knew she was hoping I'd say no. I was too upset to eat anyway."

"Did you like your classes at all?" Emily regretted the pleading tone that came out of her mouth.

"No. They put me in Algebra 1. I took that class in sixth grade."

"You passed it, right?"

Maddy glared at Emily. "I got an A. I also took two years of French and they stuck me in French 1."

"Did you tell the teachers?"

Henry put his hand on his wife's shoulder. "We'll make an appointment with the school and get it straightened out. Maybe they never received your transcripts from Chicago."

Chester rubbed against Maddy's legs. She scooped him up and slammed the door of her room behind her.

This is what teenagers do…Their brains aren't fully formed. The mantra she'd memorized from one of the stack of parenting books by her bedside failed to calm Emily this time. "The office is probably closed. I'll call the school first thing in the morning."

She shook inside. She was hoping beyond hope that the new school would be an easy transition for Maddy. Fiona must be turning over in her grave. Fiona entrusted her with her daughter and what should have been an exciting step—starting high school—was a disaster.

Chapter 12

Emily went for a quick run the next morning, relieved that her boss was still on vacation. Perhaps she could enjoy another day of teaching without the stress Mair Rose invoked. Although the course itself was more basic than she'd wanted, she was determined to sneak in some of the ideas she'd come up with over the summer—before she was handed a script and expected to play the part of unskilled labor.

Nancy met her in the mail room. "Don't forget to punch the time clock. Big brother is watching."

Emily inserted her time card, waited for the clock to read 9:01, and punched it with a flourish. "Let's see her try to dock me the minute."

"Did Maddy have a good first day at school?"

"No. She used the word *horrible* and described it as the worst day ever."

"It'll get better, you'll see."

Once Emily got in front of her class, she realized teaching this course wasn't so bad—especially since she slanted the curriculum to fit the course she'd worked on all summer. Besides, the ego boost that came from the students fawning over their professor being an award winning author made it worthwhile.

After she finished at St. Edwards, she came home to an empty cabin.

She couldn't stop think about Maddy and prayed her second day of school was going better than the first. Feeling helpless, she decided to make Maddy a favorite treat for after school. God, she herself was such a child of the seventies, with fond memories of herself and her sister coming home to a table set with fresh baked cookies and glasses of milk. Before her sister's death, their mother was devoted to them and happy keeping house and cooking meals. Afterwards, she fell into a depression and Emily and her father fended for themselves. If only she'd been paying more attention, if only she'd have taken her responsibility more seriously, things would have been so different.

She had just assembled the ingredients to make carrot cake muffins, when her phone rang.

"Winnie? Did you get safely home to Oklahoma?" Emily couldn't imagine why she was calling her.

"I know some things that might help the police solve Danielle's murder."

"Really? What things?" Again, Emily asked herself why Winnie didn't call the police directly.

"It's that boyfriend of hers—Brody Wilkerson. He was responsible for my mother's death as well as the deaths of nine other patients."

"How's that?"

"He was the engineer who installed Splash Panels-- the air conditioning units at the nursing home. It's his fault. He knew it had flaws and wasn't ready to go on the market, I'm sure of it. And Danielle defended him and his company at the trial."

"So what's that have to do with a motive for killing Danielle?"

"I don't know but I feel it in my bones. Those two were all over each other when I saw them at lunch break during the trial. It was different when I saw them at the semi-final auditions. The tension between the two of them was so thick you'd have needed a cleaver to break through it."

"Winnie, you have to talk to the police about this. I can give you the number."

"No. If Brody Wilkerson finds out I dragged his name onto the suspect list I'll be next. I probably shouldn't have called."

"Winnie? Winnie?" Emily sank into the sofa and rubbed her throbbing head. She hadn't realized Brody and Danielle were linked to Winnie over the nursing home incident. Maybe Danielle wanted Brody to admit his guilt. But then why did she defend him and his company? Henry walked in with a bakery box.

"I picked up a black forest cake for dessert. It's Maddy's favorite dessert."

"Only after caramel-mocha-chip ice cream," said Emily. "I'm glad you're home. I just got the strangest call from Winnie Cole."

"Didn't she go back home?"

"Yes, but she wanted to give me some information I guess she was too afraid to share with the police while she was here. We knew Danielle represented Splash Panels, but guess what?" She paused. "Brody Wilkerson worked for the company. He was the engineer who installed them!"

"That can't be a coincidence. Wow, Winnie had motive to kill Danielle and Brody too."

"I don't think she did it. She sounded truly frightened on the phone, and if she killed Danielle, why on earth would she call me? She'd want to disappear off the planet. That's what I'd want to do if I'd just committed a murder."

Henry pulled his phone out of his pocket and scrolled through his contacts.

"Who are you calling?"

"Someone who knows about building codes. Mike Wiles."

"Is he still with the city permits office? Susan's been trying to get him to retire ever since his heart attack."

"As far as I know. Besides, he'd still have the information." He punched in the number.

"Mike, it's Henry. We miss you, buddy. How are you and the family?"

"Good to hear your voice. We're great. Susan keeps herself busy. We're planning a trip to Disney with the grandkids next summer. And Evan's graduating medical school in May. What about you and Emily? And your daughter?"

"All good. The reason I'm calling is that there was a murder in town and it involves an engineer who worked for Splash Panels, the company that was allegedly guilty in the failure of the air conditioning unit at…"

"Yeah, I remember the case."

"Would an engineer be able to recognize a fault and how strict would the codes be?"

"The guidelines are strict, especially for something new like that, but some problems don't show up until the building's been open a little while and the systems are tested."

"Do the code inspectors ever get, you know, paid off to overlook a problem?"

"I can't say it never happens, especially when there's a rush to get a building running."

"Delays in opening are costly, right?"

"Yes, especially in the case where getting residents in means big money."

"Okay, thanks for the info. When are you and Susan coming up here? We want you to meet Maddy."

"I'm sure we'll be able to get there before winter sets in. And you know you're always welcome here in Westbrook. My love to Emily and Maddy."

Emily was in the kitchen, putting away the muffin ingredients for another day. Henry put his phone down on the counter.

"Mike thinks it's possible the code inspector could have been paid off so Nature's Vista could hurry and open with the new technology, or that the problem was so subtle it got overlooked. In any case, we have to tell the police."

"Winnie sounded genuinely afraid. I'm not sure we should say anything just yet."

Maddy came in and barely pulled the front door behind her. She tossed her backpack on the sofa.

Emily was afraid to ask. She knew by Maddy's demeanor that it had been another rough day. Henry ran into the kitchen and brought out the bakery box, dangling it in front of her.

"I picked up your favorite dessert."

"I'm not hungry." She scooped up Chester.

Emily said, "I have an idea. Let's go to the inn for dinner and you can play with Max. Maybe he can cheer you up."

Maddy's eyes brightened—or was it Emily's wishful thinking? What lame parents. Their daughter was having a miserable time adjusting to school and all they could offer was black forest cake and a chance to play with a cat.

To her surprise, Maddy said, "Okay. I can't wait to see Max."

They took Emily's Audi to the inn. The trees were turning color and beginning to blanket the roads with color. In another week or so, the tourists would be flocking here for the foliage. Having lived in New York state, Emily wasn't overly enthralled, but watching the scenery transition from green to harvest colors, to winter white added variety to her morning runs and her short commute to work.

Coralee was behind the front desk when they arrived for dinner.

"Hey, Maddy. How's school going? Max is going to be so happy to see you!"

"It's okay." She called Max and he ran to her.

"Peek out back. Noah and Franklin are almost done building the cat condo. It's quite the architectural creation."

"I thought they were building a cat tree," said Maddy.

"That's how it started. Let's just say the idea evolved."

The three of them opened the back door and saw what looked like the Swiss Family Robinson tree house.

"Wow, Max is going to love that!" said Maddy.

"I'm going to seal around the cracks and then all we have to do is sand and paint. What color do you think Max likes?" said Franklin.

"I don't know. Maybe purple, so he can feel like a king."

Henry picked up a piece of foam. "Hey, is this what you're using?" It was identical to the piece he'd found out at the cabin.

"Yeah. It's good stuff. Goes in semi-solid and dries like this so it's easy to fill in the cracks."

"Can anyone buy it?"

"They've got it down at the hardware store. Should stock it at the pet shop as well. I even used it to seal up a crack in a cat crate last week."

Emily's ears perked up. "Which cat?"

"Which cat? I dunno. Hate to say it but they all kinda look the same."

"What did the owner look like?" said Emily.

"A little older than you, dark hair, cowboy boots."

Emily and Henry said in unison, "Winnie."

Henry cleared his throat. "Franklin, do you think Winnie could have swiped some of that sealant while you weren't looking?"

"What on earth for? I mean, I suppose so. I leave it lying around pretty regularly now that I'm in repair mode."

Chapter 13

The next morning, Emily came in from her run and before she could get into the shower, Henry said, "Pat talked to Megan last night. The boot print was too big to be Winnie's. Maybe you're right and we should be looking harder at Brody."

"He was an engineer so he would have been knowledgeable enough to rig up the carbon monoxide. If he installed Splash Panels knowing there was a problem, he's responsible for those deaths at Nature's Vista. Maybe Danielle realized that after she defended him and wanted him to admit guilt."

Emily grabbed a glass of water. "That's a good guess. I have to be at work, but if you have time ..."

"I'll do what I can." He scooped oatmeal into bowls. "I hope Maddy has a better day today."

"Good morning," said Maddy, dressed in stringy jeans and a top with peek-a-boo shoulders.

Henry couldn't get used to the idea of paying money for deliberately ripped clothing, but Emily had assured him it was the style. Maddy half-heartedly ate her breakfast while rummaging through some papers in her backpack.

"Whatcha got there? Don't tell me you're studying for a test on the third day of school?"

"No, just some stupid graduation requirement. We have to document forty hours of community service in order to graduate."

"Graduate? You have four years to go." Henry filled Chester's food bowl.

"It'll take me that long to find something I want to do in this dumb town. In Chicago, I would have had a million places I could have volunteered."

Emily said, "I read in yesterday's paper that Vermont is taking in truckloads of shelter animals from the recent hurricanes in Texas and Florida. Maybe you could volunteer at the Humane Society."

"No, thanks. I hear all you do is clean dog poop when you work there."

Emily, again grateful for the calmness garnered by her morning run said, "Any way they put you to use benefits the animals. You'd be saving a dog from sleeping in a smelly cage."

Maddy rolled her eyes at her. "Speaking of smelly," Emily continued, "I'd better get in the shower or I'll be late for work. Mair Rose sent an email assuring us she'd be at her desk bright and early, expecting the same from all of us."

Emily said goodbye to Maddy, then showered and got ready for work. She wondered if she and Henry should talk to Maddy about the possibility of adoption. It might make her feel more stable—or she might blow up in one of her 'you'll never be my mother' tirades. She still walked on eggshells much of the time around Maddy, too worried about being the perfect parent and not understanding that perfect parenting was like unicorns or mermaids—they only existed in one's the imagination.

When she arrived at St. Edwards, she met Nancy in the parking lot.

"Ready for battle?" Nancy smoothed her silk skirt which matched her turquoise heels.

"Nancy, just how many pairs of shoes do you own? You look so coordinated."

"Thanks. That's a compliment, right?"

"Yes. I wish I had your sense of style. How's Brooke doing?"

"She's happy with her teachers, likes her classes. She says she's been asking Maddy to eat lunch with her but she turns her down and eats by herself."

"She's not a happy camper. They scheduled her into some classes she's already taken and she feels like everyone knows each other and she's an outsider—which she is."

"It's only the third day. It'll get better."

They walked through the side door of the stone building and into the mailroom, where one of their colleagues was crying and sweeping papers off the counter. "I quit. I really need the money, but if she won't let me have an hour off to get my ultrasound done...I don't need this stress with a baby on the way."

Nancy hugged her. "It's okay, Sasha. You're a great teacher and any school would be lucky to have you."

"Where? It's not like Sugarbury Falls is teeming with colleges, and the public schools have already started. Besides, who's going to hire a teacher who will be on maternity leave in a few months? If I didn't need the money, I'd sit home, watch soap operas, and eat candy, but Jim doesn't make enough for us to survive on his salary alone."

Emily said, "You can try tutoring. Contact the guidance counselor over at Sugarbury High. Don't juniors still have to take the SAT's? I'll bet the kind of parents we have around here will gladly pay if their child needs a good score to get into a top college."

Sasha wiped her nose with a crumpled tissue she took from the pocket of her maternity smock."

"I'm going to go to my appointment and afterwards, settle down with a cup of tea and do some serious thinking. Jim is going to be so upset. He'll want to come down here and deck Mair Rose you know." She gathered her things and left.

"Nancy, let's duck into my office for a bit. We have a little time before our classes start. I have a feeling there are things we don't know about our new boss."

Emily opened her laptop. "We already know she wasn't on the roster of what she claims was her previous job."

"Just google her. How many people do you think there are with her unusual name?"

Emily scrolled past the advertisements offering to provide background checks and criminal histories. "She worked at a public high school. Got a two out of five on ratemyteacher.com."

"That's no surprise. Keep going."

"Says she was brought up on charges of falsely accusing a teacher of mentally endangering a student. Here's something about accusing the teacher of making him stand next to the trash can because he was trash, and dangling a cross necklace over his head while chanting a prayer."

"You've got to be kidding."

"The teacher claimed it was totally untrue. The teacher was exonerated, then turned around and sued Mair."

"What was the upshot?"

"They settled out of court. Here's more. This is juicy."

"Tell me."

The phone on Emily's desk rang. "Hello, this is Dr. Fox. Yes, I'll be there."

She turned to Nancy. "It was the school. We requested a conference with the guidance counselor and they fit us in this afternoon."

"I hope they can smooth things out for Maddy. She's such a lovely girl."

"Me, too." She turned her attention back to her computer screen. "Oh…"

"What!"

"Look! It says Mair's son disappeared under mysterious circumstances. He was autistic. The ex-husband claims she killed him."

"Killed her own son?"

Emily scrolled through the article. "A body was never found and there was no ransom request. Mair said she fell asleep on the sofa and when she woke up, the front door was open and her son, Nathan, was gone. He was twelve."

"When was this?"

"About two years ago. The husband says he wasn't wearing shoes. The boy always wore one particular pair of sneakers and they were still in his closet. The kid was obsessive-compulsive about getting dirty and the father said there's no way he would have gone outside without his shoes. And he claims the area rug in the living room was missing."

"She was never charged? Why would she kill her own son?"

"The father says she had no patience for Nathan, especially since he'd become a tween. She went on and on about sending him to an institution but the father wouldn't have it."

"Infanticide. That's heavy duty messed up."

"I don't know what they call it, but yes, it's really messed up… and I think I have an idea for my next true crime book."

Chapter 14

Even after stopping by Maddy's school, Emily arrived home before Henry or Maddy. She sat with her laptop, intrigued by her new story idea. She found that Mair and her husband divorced shortly after their son's disappearance. Without too much effort, she determined Mair's ex still lived in the area and she jotted down his phone number. She had her phone in her hand when it began to vibrate.

"Winnie? Is everything okay?"

"Did they arrest Brody?"

"Not yet, why?"

"I remembered something Danielle said. She mentioned thinking Brody was cheating on her because he was taking phone calls in private and running out to late night meetings."

"Was he cheating?"

"No, it turned out to be business but Danielle was worried. She said it couldn't have been on the up and up if he was meeting in secret late at night."

"Did she mention a name?"

"Just that he was in cahoots with a partner who was planning on making them both a fortune. I thought it might help."

"A partner? I thought he was just the engineer behind the project."

"He was more than that. Splash Panels was his baby."

"It's another lead, but why don't you call the police directly?"

"They'll try to get me to come back to Vermont and I can't. My sister is having some health issues and I don't want to leave her alone."

"I hope she gets better soon. I'll pass along the information."

Henry threw his keys on the table and sat down next to Emily on the sofa.

"I didn't hear you come in."

"You were pretty engrossed in your phone call."

"It was Winnie. She told me Danielle had mentioned Brody had a partner. If Danielle found out and threatened to blow the secret…"

"He'd have motive to kill her. Interesting. Brody *and* the partner had motive. I was talking to Pat earlier and he mentioned Danielle's parents are back and coming into town tomorrow to speak with the detectives and take home her things. I wonder if they know anything about it."

"Danielle's parents are coming tomorrow? I told Kurt after it happened I'd go over and gather her things together before they showed up. Want to come with me after dinner and do it?"

Henry agreed, then went into the kitchen and poured himself a glass of iced tea. Emily followed him.

"The school fixed Maddy's schedule. She should be happier. They're moving her to Geometry and French 2." Emily took some store bought oatmeal cookies out of the cabinet and arranged them on a plate. Maddy would be home any minute.

"I'll bet Maddy can get through high school in three years, maybe less. I started college when I was sixteen. It'll give her a head start on veterinary school."

Emily said, "Did she say she wanted to go to veterinary school?"

"Not in so many words, but with her mind…"

Maddy came in and plopped her backpack on the recliner. She had dark circles under her eyes and her hair was tousled from the open windows on the school bus.

"How was your day?" asked Emily. She already knew the answer. "There are cookies on the table."

"It was okay. They said I'll be starting my new classes tomorrow." Maddy went into the kitchen and poured a glass of Almond milk. Emily and Henry followed her. "I have to do this stupid assignment for Social Studies. We're supposed to make a family tree and come up with a coat of arms."

Emily said, "Your mom was born in Scotland. I don't know anything about your dad, except when Fiona chose a donor, I'm sure she requested he have a similar background. You look every bit as Scottish as Fiona did." Emily thought what she said came out sounding idiotic, but she was grasping at straws. She hadn't even seen Fiona since college.

"I have an idea," said Henry. "They have those kits now where you can trace your ancestry through your DNA."

"No thanks," said Maddy. "The assignment's due at the end of the week."

"I know Fiona had a brother who still lived in Scotland, at least back when we were in college. She'd get an occasional call from him."

"Uncle Malcolm," said Maddy. "He used to send me birthday cards when I was little. He stopped sending them years ago. I don't want to make a big deal over this. It's not like the teacher can check or anything. Henry, can I just pretend you're my father and use your family tree?"

Henry flushed. "I'd be incredibly flattered. My father was born in England but his family came over to the states when he was nine. My mother was born in

New York. An immigrant story…" He was slightly hurt when she cut him off.

"Great. I'll use that. I can fill in the other half of the tree with my real mom." She ate the cookies, scooped up Chester, and retreated into her room.

Emily opened the fridge. "How about I make black bean chili for dinner, then we can swing by the cabin and pack Danielle's things?"

Henry sat at the table, head leaning on his hand. "Huh?"

"You look like you're a million miles away. Is chili okay for dinner?"

"Sure."

"What are you thinking so seriously about?"

Henry picked up his head and looked into her eyes. "Remember what we started talking about the other day? I want to adopt Maddy. I know we chose not to have children, but we got a second chance when Maddy came into our lives. I love her, Emily. I already feel like her father and I want to make it legal."

"I love her, too. I'm not sure how great of a mother I am, though. I feel so inept at times."

"I think all parents feel that way. I know I thought my parents knew nothing about anything during my teen years, but it's normal, right? It didn't mean I didn't love them, and in the end, I realized they were smarter and wiser than I gave them credit for."

"You don't think it's too soon after her mother's death?"

"We can ask. If she says no, it really doesn't change anything. We'll still be a family."

Emily drained a can of beans and tossed an onion to Henry to chop. She thought about the time she'd already spent with Maddy, shopping, caring for Chester, helping her through the sad times when she cried over photos of Fiona. She loved going out to dinner at the inn, the three of them—like a family. But so many times she felt like she didn't know what to say or how to act around her. Was she good enough to be someone's mother? She certainly wasn't a very good sister, and she wasn't a good enough daughter to pull her mother out of her depression.

"Em, what do you think? You're so good with Maddy."

There were those times Maddy screamed at her about how she wasn't her real mother; the times Maddy slammed her door and locked herself in her room, making Emily feel helpless...She thought with her mind, but gave into her heart. "Okay. Let's do it."

Chapter 15

After dinner, they knocked on Kurt's door and followed him to the rental cabin. When they walked in, Emily shivered, remembering the sight of Danielle lying dead on the floor the previous time they were here.

"You can pull the door shut when you leave. I'll lock it back up when I take Prancer for his bedtime walk."

"Thanks, Kurt. It shouldn't take us long to gather her things." Emily locked the pine door from the inside.

"Well, should we start in the kitchen?" said Henry. "I doubt much of anything in there belonged to her." He opened the wooden cabinets and drawers, seeing standard kitchen fare. "Nothing but pots and pans, plates, silverware…"

"Kurt stocked all that for when Chloe came." Emily headed into the bedroom and pulled clothing out of the cedar scented drawers and closet. Danielle's suitcases were still lying open on the floor next to the canopy bed.

Henry started in the master bathroom. "I wish we'd gotten the chance over dinner to ask Maddy how she feels about us adopting her."

"I know. She was in a rush to finish her homework and on a rant about her teachers. It wasn't good timing." When she finished packing the clothes, she found Danielle's laptop tangled in with the comforter. She gingerly touched a key and a letter popped up on the screen. *"Put another ten thousand in the account by*

Friday or you know what will happen." A cold chill traveled up her spine.

Henry said, "I can throw away the open shampoo and used soap, right?"

"Henry, come quick. You have to see this. Danielle was blackmailing someone."

Henry looked over her shoulder. "Who was this intended for? And what information did she have that was so valuable?"

Emily rifled through the nightstand and rummaged through the top dresser drawer.

"What are you looking for?"

"I'm not sure. Some kind of clue as to who she was blackmailing." She looked under the bed and pulled out a briefcase. She flipped through the papers.

"Did you find something?"

"Yeah. A business card. Wallace Hartman Investments—why does that name sound familiar?"

Henry thought for a minute. "The owner of the assisted living place was Wallace Hartman! I read it on line when I was researching the story Winnie told you."

The floor creaked. Emily jumped. "What was that noise?"

"Just the cabin adjusting to the cold weather. Floorboards are contracting."

"And that? Who's banging against the wall? I'm scared."

"Probably just an animal outside. Refocus. Was Danielle blackmailing Brody, or Wallace Hartman?"

"Over what? She won the case for Splash Panels. If the company wasn't at fault, then Nature's Vista was twice removed from being at fault. Unless…maybe she found out Splash Panels knew it wasn't ready for marketing and Hartman pushed to go ahead anyway *after* the trials were over."

The cabin went dark. Emily screamed and grabbed Henry's hand, not allowing herself to breathe.

Henry reached into his jacket pocket for his phone and found the flashlight app. "There, it's okay. The wind probably knocked down the power line. We'll stop by Kurt's and let him know."

Emily screamed again. "Henry, that was the front door slamming shut. I locked it from the inside. Call the police."

Henry fumbled with his phone. "There's no service. Wait here."

"Don't leave me alone."

"Let me make sure they're gone." He crept into the living room, listening for the prowler. His fists were clenched so tightly that his fingers felt numb. He hugged the wall, looking up and down, left and right. Creeping noiselessly, he went into the kitchen. A flood of light blinded him. Headlights glared through the kitchen window illuminating the room like a stadium at a night game. Screeching wheels like nails on a chalkboard assaulted his ears. Catching his breath, he said, "Emily, he's gone. Come on out."

Emily exhaled. "I heard a car. Who do you think it was? Brody?"

"As far as we know he's in Falls Church. We'll stop at the police station." Henry opened the kitchen door and saw skid marks in the dirt. "I'll bet the police can take a tire impression. It may help them find the creep." He noticed something hanging on the outside wall. "The fuse box isn't shut all the way." Using his phone flashlight, he pulled it open and moved the levers."

"The lights are back on." Emily allowed herself a much needed breath.

"The fuse box was deliberately tampered with. Someone didn't want us snooping through Danielle's things."

"Henry, look." She pointed to the ground at a half smoked cigarette. "Should I pick it up with a tissue?"

"Leave it there. The police will be coming out and it may be more helpful if it's left where it fell."

They got back into the Jeep and drove to the station. Emily clutched Henry's free hand. The wind, sounding like a ghost in the dark, whipped through the partially opened windows. Her cheeks stung from the brisk night air.

Emily's stomach did somersaults as Henry sped along the dark, twisty, mountain road. Time passed in slow motion. Her fight or flight reflex was still in high gear when she spotted a cruiser parked in front of the illuminated police station. They ran through the station door.

"Detective Wooster, we have something to report," said Emily, trying to catch her breath. Detective Wooster was Megan's partner and looked like a young Ron Howard.

Emily and Henry spat out the details. "We were packing Danielle's things since her parents are coming in tomorrow. We heard a noise, which Henry thought was just an animal. Then the lights went out and…"

"We heard the door slam and I saw headlights through the kitchen window. The fuse box had been tampered with."

Detective Wooster said, "I'll call Megan and head over there. Go home and lock your door. It was probably a burglar looking for electronics."

Henry put his arm around Emily and led her back to the Jeep. She rested against his shoulder as he drove home. When they walked into their cabin, Maddy immediately ran and grabbed onto them.

"Maddy, what's wrong?" said Emily. "You're trembling."

"I...I. I tried to call you. Someone was peeking through the window right after you left. I was so scared. I locked myself in my room with Chester."

"Why didn't you call the police?" Emily was inadvertently yelling.

Henry stroked her arm. "Maddy, I'll call them now. We were at Kurt's cabin and someone else was there too. I'll bet it was the same person." Henry went outside and walked around, making sure all the windows were secure. Next to Maddy's window, he saw something on the ground—a partially smoked cigarette.

Chapter 16

The next morning, Henry, Emily, and Maddy sat together at the table. Henry had made scrambled eggs.

"Do you think the police caught whoever was here last night? What do you think he wanted?" Maddy looked at Henry, then Emily.

"We found a blackmail note on Danielle's computer. I think whoever she was blackmailing was there looking for whatever she had on him. That reminds me, in all the commotion last night, I forgot to tell the police about the blackmail letter and Wallace Hartman's business card. Wallace Hartman owns Nature's Vista."

"So you think this nursing home owner killed Danielle and was spying on me?" said Maddy.

Emily didn't have an answer. "I don't know. Danielle's parents are coming in today. Maybe they'll shed some light on the situation." She looked at the rooster clock. "I have a few minutes. Maddy, Henry and I want to talk to you about something."

"Sounds serious. Are you worried the prowler is coming back?"

"No," said Henry. "The police are onto him. He'd be stupid to try again." Henry cleared his throat. "Emily and I were talking, actually we've been talking about this for a while." He fidgeted with his Fitbit.

"What he's trying to say is," said Emily, "Henry and I would like to adopt you. We want to officially become a family." She held her breath, thinking how lame she just sounded. She looked at Maddy for a hint of a response.

After an uncomfortable silence, Maddy said, "I don't know what to say. Not that I don't appreciate what you two have been doing for me..."

Henry said, "You don't have to tell us right now. Emily and I love you, Maddy. That won't change no matter what your answer." He felt a gnawing in his stomach as he watched Maddy grab her backpack and head for the school bus.

"I think she was open to the idea," said Emily. "She needs time to process it, that's all."

"Well, like I said, it won't really change anything." He couldn't finish his breakfast. "I have to get over to the hospital. Have a good day at work."

Emily cleared the dishes and turned off the coffee maker. She knew how much Henry was hoping Maddy would jump for joy at the adoption offer. She herself was ready to take the next step. In actuality, she felt Maddy should be grateful they'd taken her in and wanted to call her their daughter. She should have appreciated the offer and jumped at the chance to be legally part of their family. After all, if they hadn't rescued her, she'd be living in some foster home. She drove to work, and again ran into Nancy in the parking lot.

"Emily, you look exhausted," said Nancy.

"We had quite the night. I'll fill you in later."

"I did some more digging on our friend Mair. Guess what? Mair's father is a retired detective. I was reading an interview with Mair's ex and he claimed his ex-father-in-law covered up the murder and that's why they never found a body. If you are serious about writing that new book, you should go talk to the ex."

"I was thinking I would as soon as I get things settled at home. Maddy's schedule got changed. Hopefully she'll be happier."

"Hope so. Did you notice how Mair doesn't have a single family photo on her desk or anywhere in her office?"

"I did. At first I figured she had no family—after all, who would live with her?"

Emily and Nancy walked into the mail room, where an elderly woman with glasses was stuffing mail into faculty boxes. The smell from the copier gave Emily a headache.

The woman paused. "Emily, did that guy with the beret ever find you?"

"What guy?"

"I was here late catching up day before yesterday and I ran into an older gentleman I'd never seen before. At least I think he was older. His hair was gray. He said he was the father of one of your students and needed to speak to you. He wouldn't leave his name."

"Really? This isn't elementary school, and the semester's just starting. I wonder what that was all about."

"If he really needs to see you, he'll be back." She continued stuffing boxes.

Emily felt uneasy and it wasn't just from the headache. Someone stalked them at Danielle's cabin last night, someone peered into their windows when Maddy was home alone, and now an elderly gentleman wearing a beret was looking for her. Elderly gentleman—that wasn't Brody. She taught her morning class, then brainstormed ideas for her new book. While working on an outline, Henry called.

"Hey, Em, do you want to meet me at the inn for lunch? Pat says Danielle's parents are in town."

"Did the police interview them already?"

"Yeah, first thing this morning."

"Give me a few minutes and I'll meet you there."

Emily finished her notes, then googled Wallace Hartman. Could he be in town looking for her? A photo would help. She scrolled down the screen. Hartman owned Nature's Vista as well as two other assisted living facilities. She found a bio and a photo. Hartman was bald, not gray like the secretary described the man in the beret. Multiple rolls of fat piles supported his chin like a pillow. It was unlikely he'd have been capable of climbing roofs and stuffing a chimney.

On the way to the inn, Emily wondered if the gentleman claiming to be a parent was the same one who broke into Danielle's and spied on Maddy. For that matter, was he also Danielle's murderer? Her stomach growled as she'd barely eaten breakfast this morning.

The inn was slightly busier than it had been the past couple of weeks. Max was perched on top of the front desk, soaking in the sun that shone through the front doors. Emily spotted Henry, seated near a window overlooking the porch.

"Hey, Em. Over here." He got up and gave her a kiss. "I've eaten most of the rolls that were in the basket, but we can get more. You okay?"

"Yeah, just hungry." Head now pounding, Emily couldn't decide if eating would make her feel better or worse. She opted for minestrone soup and a rustic salad with heirloom tomatoes. Henry, teetering on becoming vegetarian like the rest of his family, ordered a spinach frittata with baked fries.

"Henry, someone *is* stalking us. The lady who works in the office said a man was looking for me the other day."

"Have you been leaving your wedding ring at home again?"

"Seriously. It's most likely the same man who spied on us at the cabin and the one who scared Maddy."

"Brody?"

"He had gray hair and the secretary referred to him as older."

"Wallace Hartman?"

Emily pulled out her phone and showed Henry the picture she'd found.

"Nope, not Wallace Hartman."

Coralee, always the hostess, stopped by their table. "How's the food today?"

"Delicious as always," said Emily. "Did you meet Danielle's parents? We heard they are staying here."

Coralee pointed to the next table. "That's them. I don't even know what to say to them."

"What can you say that doesn't sound hollow?" After all these years, she still shuddered when she remembered all the *we're praying for you* and *she's with God and not suffering anymore* comments that were meant to make her family feel better after her sister died. A simple *sorry for your loss* would have been enough.

"They're leaving tomorrow." Coralee wiped her hands on her pinafore.

"I'll talk to them and arrange a time to bring over Danielle's things."

When they'd finished eating, they approached the LaPierre's. "Excuse me," said Emily. "You're Danielle's parents, right? We're sorry for your loss."

Mrs. LaPierre looked at her blankly. "Yes. Did you know Danielle?"

"We're friends of the man whose cabin she rented. I was asked to gather up her things and I wondered when would be a good time to bring them over."

Danielle's father, tall and lanky with the same blond hair as his daughter said, "Anytime. We aren't going anywhere today."

Emily sat in the empty chair. "The detectives are working hard to find your daughter's killer. Were you close to her boyfriend, Brody? He must be taking her death hard."

Mrs. LaPierre said, "He was no longer her boyfriend. Danielle defended him at the trial and after that things went south. She regretted defending him, and in fact, that was the last criminal case she did before switching into estate law."

"She's been—I mean, she was—working for an international firm. Paid better and the hours weren't so crazy," said her father.

Emily said, "Do you think she uncovered something that angered someone enough to murder her?"

Mrs. LaPierre's eyes teared. "All she said was something about the whole thing being a farce. The testimony from residents' families about how their loved ones died from the heat kept her up at night. Danielle was very close to her own grandmother and the story hit her hard."

"Even though she defended Splash Panels?"

"When she was working on the trial, she believed it was all an accident. After they won, she had second thoughts." Mr. LaPierre put his arm around his wife. "Brody was always scheming to make a buck. Danielle found out he had invested money in Splash Panels and had a lot riding on the system being up and ready to operate."

"In other words," said Mr. LaPierre, "he cut corners on preliminary testing."

Coralee came to the table. "On your way out, would you like to see Max, Danielle's cat? I thought you might want to take him home with you, though we'd miss him terribly."

Emily hadn't considered the idea of Danielle's parents whisking Max away from Sugarbury Falls. Her stomach ached thinking of how painful it would be for Coralee, and especially for Maddy.

"No," said Mr. LaPierre. "I have terrible allergies. Had to pop a few Zyrtec every time we visited Danielle. I'm sure he's happy here."

"Happy as a clam. He gets lots of attention from the guests. If you're sure you can't take him..." Coralee's eyes sparkled.

"Danielle would be thrilled her cat is living out his life as the Outside Inn mascot. We appreciate you giving him a home."

Emily and Henry said their goodbyes. Her heart ached for the LaPierres, who would never experience the sweet events of Danielle's future—marriage, grandchildren, professional success. How would they ever get over the loss? On the way to the parking lot, Emily's phone rang.

"Yes, thanks for getting back to us so soon. Really? Okay, then I guess we'll have to keep looking."

Henry put his hand on his wife's shoulder. "What was that all about?"

"It was Detective Wooster. They lifted prints off of the fuse box at the cabin. They aren't Brody's."

Chapter 17

After lunch, Emily went back to her office and saw the list she'd brainstormed earlier. She grabbed a legal pad and started making a preliminary outline of her new book. Needing more background information, she took a chance and called Mair's ex-husband, hoping he would be willing to talk to her.

She looked up the number, took a deep breath, and made the call. "Mr. Rose, this is Emily Fox. I'm a true crime writer and I was hoping to interview you for a book I'm planning to write on your son's disappearance. With your permission, of course."

"For the past two years no one's shown much interest. They say he wandered off and since they didn't find a body, that was the end of it."

"I'm hoping to draw attention to the case and renew interest."

"Mair's father is on the force, or at least he was. He blocked the investigation from the start. I'll help you any way I can. My son disappeared without a trace and I want to nail my ex-wife. I'm positive she killed him. Even her story about falling asleep on the sofa didn't ring true. She never, ever fell asleep by day. She guarded against it because she was an insomniac and did everything she could not to stay awake all night."

"Tell me what you think happened."

"The police didn't find any traces of blood, but they ignored the fact that the area carpet had been removed. I think she wrapped his body in it and disposed of him before I got home."

"How do you think she killed him?"

"He was big for a twelve-year-old, and strong, too. I think she poisoned him. I told the police that there was a huge bottle of juice, you know the kind—so heavy they wrap a plastic handle around the opening so you can carry it?"

"Like the ones you get at Costco, right?"

"Yeah. It was in the fridge that morning. Nathan gulped that stuff like it was water, but even at that, there's no way he went through an entire bottle by the afternoon. It was gone when they searched the house later that day."

Emily frantically took notes as she listened. "And without a body, poisoning couldn't be proven. Did you look for the juice bottle?"

"By the time I thought of it, the trash had been picked up. If only we could find his body, perhaps it's not too late to test his remains. I don't know what she did with him. He was pretty heavy, so she must have had a time of it dragging his body out."

"Or, she poisoned him, got him in the car, and took him to another location until the poison killed him." She jotted that on her legal pad and marked it with an asterisk.

"I checked the gas in her car. I'd filled it the day before and the needle hadn't moved. The police sent divers into Lake Pleasant, and volunteers searched the woods for days. Without a body, we can't prove murder."

"What did you have at home that was potentially fatal?" Emily doodled on the legal pad while she waited for an answer.

"Mair took sleeping pills, for the insomnia. And I had gasoline and antifreeze in the garage, but those containers were intact."

Emily looked at the clock on her desk. "I'm sorry, but I have to teach a class in a few minutes. Do you mind if we talk again?"

"Mind? If you can stir up interest, perhaps the police will reopen the case. Are you a mother? If so, then you know you would work until your dying day searching for your child."

"Yes, I have a daughter and you're right. I'd never stop looking."

Emily walked to class tossing around ideas. Where would Mair have hidden the body of a twelve-year-old if not the lake or the surrounding woods? Would she have used her prescription sleeping pills to kill him? It would have been difficult to save enough of them if she was using them herself. What about the shoes? The father said his son would never go outside without shoes, so if he was drugged, would he have still insisted on wearing shoes?

While teaching, Emily was distracted both by the mystery of Mair's son's disappearance, and by her conversation with Danielle's parents. Who was Danielle blackmailing? The likely candidates were Brody and Hartman. Brody claimed he wasn't in Sugarbury Falls before Danielle died and there wasn't evidence to contradict his story. He hadn't purchased plane or train tickets and his car didn't show up on toll cameras.

"Mrs. Fox, can you check this over?" said a twenty something student. They were working on putting together a descriptive paragraph.

Emily took his paper. *The plane was stocked with wine and endless trays of Brie, artisan bread and grapes as big as plums. The leather seats freely turned...*

"Private plane!" Did she say that out loud?

"Is it okay? You said we could describe anything."

"Yes, yes, it's fine. Good job. Keep going." Emily couldn't wait to call the detectives. Why hadn't she thought of it before? If Brody was working with Hartman, perhaps he hitched a ride on a private plane!

"Okay, class. Finish up your paragraphs and post to the group. Respond to two of your classmates." She quickly shoved her things into her tote bag and exited ahead of some of the stragglers. She couldn't wait to get home and check out Hartman to see if he owned a plane, and to talk to Megan. She went straight to the parking lot and into her Audi. She pushed the speed limit once she hit the main road.

In her rearview mirror, she spotted a white car with tinted windows. She'd seen the same car back at the college parking lot. Was it following her? She made a sharp left turn and the car turned right behind her. The car's windows were tinted and Emily couldn't see the driver. Not wanting to lead him to her house, she took the long way into town and pulled in front of the police station. That's when the car sped off, before she could catch the plate number.

Emily walked into the station. "May I see Detective Wooster or Detective O'Leary?"

Detective O'Leary came out of her office. "Emily, what can I do for you?"

"A white car with tinted windows followed me all the way from St. Edwards."

"Come in." She opened the counter and led them to her office. "What was the make and model? Did you see the driver or get any of the numbers off the license plate?"

"No to both and I'm not even sure of the make and model; it was a newish, non-descript sedan."

"Any idea who may have had a reason to follow you?"

"No…well maybe. Someone at work said an elderly gentleman claiming to be a student's father was looking for me, but he didn't leave a note or come back."

"You and Henry were followed to Danielle's cabin the other night, and you said someone had been peeking in the windows of your home. Chances are it's the same person."

Emily said, "I was wondering if you can check the private flights coming into our area around the time Danielle was killed. I think Brody was friendly with the owner of Nature's Vista, Wallace Hartman. And if Hartman owned a plane…"

"Sure, I can do that. Wallace Hartman—they did a piece on *Sixty Minutes* about him."

"Danielle's parents said Brody and Hartman both had a vested interest in the success of Splash Panels. Perhaps he pushed Brody to install the system despite potential flaws, and maybe he was even bribing Brody. Or, they were equally guilty of rushing it to market. After the trial, Danielle found out Splash Panels was responsible for those deaths at Nature's Vista and was blackmailing someone. It could have been either one of them."

Megan O'Leary clicked through her desktop computer until she found what she needed.

"Yes, Hartman owns a private plane. And that plane landed here two days before Danielle LaPierre's death."

Chapter 18

When Emily arrived home, she changed into yoga pants and a soft t-shirt. By the time she came downstairs, Henry was working on the Sudoku he'd saved from the morning newspaper. Chester sat on the back of the sofa, over Henry's head.

"How was your afternoon?" said Henry.

"Informative. I starting outlining my new book, then spoke to Mair's ex-husband."

"That was quick. Did you learn anything you can use?"

"He's sure she killed their son."

"Without a body, it's hard to prove."

"Mair didn't have oodles of time to kill her son, clean up, and dispose of the body. Her son Nathan came home from school around three. Mair's ex came home from work around six. If she moved the body, it couldn't have been far. The needle on the gas tank hadn't moved according to her ex. He had filled the tank the day before."

"So maybe she's telling the truth and he just wandered out."

"No, the ex-husband says things don't add up. There was a missing jug of juice, the area rug had disappeared, Mair claims to have been napping which her ex says she never does, and Nathan never went outside without shoes."

Chester leaped off the sofa and ran to the door when Maddy walked in. She plopped her backpack down and sat in between Emily and Henry, something she rarely if ever did.

"I have an idea for my community service project. I was reading about a cat café out in California. People come in, have coffee and pastry, and play with the cats, who are shelter animals. They can adopt a cat right then and there. There's one out in St. Louis that takes reservations, it's so popular."

Emily was thrilled to see Maddy so animated. "That's a wonderful idea. Out of sight, out of mind, but when the cats are visible they're much more likely to be given a home."

"Lovely idea, but I'm afraid we don't have the room to make a cat café here. I'm sure there are zoning laws and licenses to apply for," said Henry. He envisioned them converting his woodworking studio into a play room for cats and he was ready to defend his ground.

"No," said Maddy. "I was thinking about the inn. Coralee says all the time how much the guests love having Max there, and look at that great cat condo Franklin and Noah built."

Emily said, "I'm sure there are laws about having animals around the food."

"They don't have to be allowed in the dining room. I did some research. Suppose Coralee converts the back porch area into the cat area. Guests can purchase their food, then carry it out there and play with the cats. The homeless cats would be in a position to find a loving new home."

"Well, I told you they brought in truckloads of shelter animals when Texas and Florida went through those hurricanes. I think it's a great idea, but don't get your hopes up until you talk to Coralee," said Emily.

"I won't. I'm going to come up with a few designs." She hugged Emily and then Henry before going to her room, surprising them both since she'd shown little if any physical affection toward them ever. The landline, which they barely used, startled them with its metallic ring. Emily made her way to the phone.

"Hello. Hello." She tapped the receiver. "Whoever it was hung up."

"Do you think it was Winnie again?"

"No, she calls my cell. I rarely give out the house number."

"Probably a wrong number, or a telemarketer." He tried to sound reassuring, but had his own doubts. The house phone rarely rang at all.

"That older gentleman claiming to be a student's father was looking for me at work; remember I told you at lunch?"

"Yes, did he come back after lunch?"

"No, but after I left you, a white car followed me."

"Followed you where?"

"To the police station, as it turns out. I wasn't about to lead him here. I spoke to Megan and she thinks it's the same person who followed us to Danielle's cabin and spooked Maddy by looking in the windows."

"You could have been kidnapped or even killed! What else did Megan say?"

"They're going to work on it. Then, I asked about the possibility that Brody flew into town to kill Danielle on a private plane. She looked up Wallace Hartman and he owns a plane. She said she'd check the executive airport."

"My head's spinning. Let's get dinner started, I'm hungry." Henry opened the fridge. "There are eggs and some moldy green peppers in here. I say we go to Coralee's. It'll give Maddy a chance to pitch her cat café idea, too." He tossed the rotten peppers into the garbage disposal.

Maddy was more animated than Emily had ever seen her. If it took creating a cat café to make her happy, she'd change the litterboxes herself. When they walked into the lobby of the inn, Max was sitting on the front desk, as if waiting for Maddy. The aroma of fresh bread made Emily's stomach rumble. Coralee came in from the dining area.

"You picked a good night. I'm making an acorn squash casserole as we speak. I have to say, Maddy, you have certainly gotten me to expand my vegetarian menu and the guests seem to love it."

Maddy smiled as she stroked Max. "Coralee, at school we have to do a community service project as a graduation requirement. You know how you said the guests love Max?"

"They sure do, and I can't say I mind the company."

"What do you think of converting the porch into a cat café? The guests could bring food into the area and play with shelter cats."

Coralee said, "Well, sounds intriguing. Not sure about using the porch though. I like keeping it open for the guests to rock and enjoy a good read when the weather permits it."

Franklin, who'd been repairing a crack in the wall, said, "We could use the extra room off the dining area. It's supposed to be a banquet room, but I haven't yet seen it used."

"No," said Coralee. "When we do a private booking I generally just close the dining room to the public. The banquet room is dreary without any windows. Doesn't happen often as it is."

"I could help the young lady," said Franklin. "And I'll bet Noah would help, too. We've just about finished the cat condo."

"I'll have to see what kind of regulations exist," said Coralee.

Henry interrupted. "No, let Maddy handle looking up the regulations. It's her project—shouldn't give you extra work."

"And I'll go over to the shelter and see how they like the idea. We can call it Coralee's Cat Café."

Coralee said, "Hmmm, I'm thinking we could buy some cushy furniture and Franklin and Noah can build some tables. We could even decorate with local crafts!"

"Sounds cozy," said Emily.

"That's it!" said Coralee. "Coralee's Cozy Cat Café."

"I love the name," said Emily. Henry and Franklin nodded.

Coralee seated them at a table overlooking the porch. Emily and Maddy opted to try the squash casserole, while Henry ordered baked scrod. Over dinner, Maddy talked a blue streak about ideas for the cat café.

"Maybe we can get some artist to paint a mural— maybe a jungle scene."

"You can set up a basket for cat food donations," said Emily.

"And a percentage of food sales could go directly to the shelter—if it's okay with Coralee," said Henry.

They ordered apple pie a la mode for dessert and were stuffed by the time they got up to leave.

Megan and Pat, holding hands, walked into the lobby as the Foxes were exiting.

"Try the squash casserole," said Emily. "It's to die for."

Megan said, "I did some research. Wallace Hartman did file a flight plan. I confirmed that the plane arrived two days before the murder, and returned the morning you found the body."

Emily clapped her hands together. "Wallace Hartman killed Danielle! She was blackmailing him and he hunted her down."

"Wallace Hartman wasn't on the plane, but guess who was?" said Megan. "You were right in the first place—Brody Wilkerson."

Chapter 19

Over breakfast the next morning, Henry and Emily went over what they'd learned from Megan. Brody had been in town at the time of Danielle's murder and lied about it. He was working with Wallace Hartman from Nature's Vista who had a large investment in Splash Panels. They both had a lot to gain by the successful implementation of Splash Panels at Nature's Vista, since it was the first facility to use the new system.

Emily filled Chester's bowl. "If Brody stayed at the inn, Coralee would have recognized him. I'll bet he stayed at the Aster Inn down the street."

"Even if he did, there's no evidence placing him in Danielle's cabin the night she was killed. It's too bad there were no witnesses."

"Wait," said Emily. "Did the detectives knock on doors and ask?"

"What doors? I don't even know who moved into the place on the other side of Kurt's. Anyhow, I'm sure Megan and Ron will follow up on it."

Maddy, wearing a new hot pink blouse and jeans, poured herself a bowl of cereal. "Do we have any more almond milk?"

"You're in a good mood," said Henry. "Nice to see you smiling."

"I was thinking about the cat café all night. I was too excited to sleep. I'm going to get my guidance counselor to approve it today, then I'll start checking out rules and if we need a permit."

"If you need help let me know. Do you want a copy of the Sudoku?"

"Yes, thanks." Maddy ate every bit of her breakfast, grabbed her backpack, and on the way out the door said, "By the way, I do want to be adopted. By the two of you, I mean."

The door closed and Henry looked at Emily. "Did she just say she wants us to adopt her?"

"That's what it sounded like to me. We're officially going to be parents." Emily's stomach fluttered. This is what they wanted, but she suddenly felt more pressure than ever to fill Fiona's shoes. Her class wasn't until later, so she decided a run would help clear her head.

The first official cold front had moved in the previous night and Emily savored the feeling of chilly air on her face as she ran. Today she opted for the route which took her past Kurt's and around Lake Pleasant. She occasionally saw Franklin the handyman out on a walk, or often Kurt and Prancer were up and about. Today she spotted two new faces—three if you counted the adorable black Border Collie accompanying them.

The two women, both in their thirties as far as she could estimate, smiled at her, and she stopped to say hello, wondering if they were visitors or new neighbors. The one holding the leash was short, with dark hair pulled into a ponytail. She wore a Yale hoodie.

The dog barked at Emily, then immediately responded to the command to sit. "He's very sweet once he gets to know you. I'm Rebecca and this is my wife, Abby."

Abby's light brown hair reached to the middle of her back and she wore a Patriot's sweat jacket. She extended her hand. "Do you live around here? We moved in a few weeks ago."

"Yes, just around the bend. I'm Emily Fox. You must have bought the place next to Kurt Olav. Have you met him yet?"

Abby said, "The guy with the black lab? We've run into him a few times."

"If you need anything, let me know. I'm a writer/college professor over at St. Edwards. We live down there." She pointed in the direction of her house. "Are you both working here?"

Rebecca said, "Abby's a freelance photographer and I do security for BizTech. We can both work pretty much anywhere. We vacationed here last summer and fell in love with the place." The wind picked up and she pulled up the hood of her sweatshirt.

Emily thought about inviting them over for dinner but didn't want to appear overly eager to get to know them. After all, most of Sugarbury Falls' residents treasured their privacy. "It's so nice to meet you both. I'd better get going." Emily started to jog, then turned around. "By any chance, have you noticed anyone lurking around the cabin next to yours over the past few weeks?"

"We heard there was a murder, but we haven't seen anything. The detectives already questioned us."

"Okay, just thought I'd ask." She turned and ran back home.

*****

While Emily finished her run, Henry went off to the hospital and was immediately recruited by a colleague to consult on a difficult case. Since moving to Sugarbury Falls, his days mostly consisted of diagnosing the flu or confirming the occasional broken bone, so he welcomed the challenge.

By midmorning, the emergency room had cleared out and he wandered over to his computer. Loving a puzzle, he searched for a connection between Brody

Wilkerson, Wallace Hartman, and anyone else who had a stake in Splash Panels. He didn't hear his buddy come up behind him.

"You look busy," said Pat.

Henry jumped. "You trying to give me a heart attack or what?" He caught his breath. "Things are quiet and I'm bored. I'm trying to connect the dots in Danielle's murder. Brody Wilkerson was in town the day Danielle was murdered, and lied to the police about it. I think Danielle was blackmailing him and he came to kill her."

"Megan said there wasn't any physical evidence placing him at the cabin. No fingerprints, no witnesses…"

"It's the only logical conclusion I can come up with. Who else had a motive?"

"What about the owner? We don't know the note was meant for Brody, it could have been for the owner of the business. There were some unidentified prints at the place, after eliminating Kurt's of course."

Henry searched Wallace Hartman. After digging through numerous pages of hits, he found an online interview from around the time Splash Panels debuted. He read through it quickly.

"Pat, this guy owned Nature's Vista, but was a major investor in Splash Panels. He had a huge stake in its success. Not only did he own other nursing homes, he had connections with businesses all over the country ready to purchase Splash Panels for themselves if it was successful. He stood to make a fortune."

"So Danielle knew this and was blackmailing him, or Brody was stalking her and wound up killing her. Did I miss something? Who actually owns Splash Panels?"

"That's the million-dollar question. Henry looked at the empty emergency waiting room and knew he wouldn't be missed if he stepped out for an hour or so. "How about taking a ride for an early lunch? Let's check the Aster Inn and see if anyone saw Brody the night of Danielle's murder. I'll drive."

They jumped into his Jeep.

"Pat, you owe me a cigar."

"Emily's pregnant? No way!"

"Really? Where did you get your medical license? That ship has sailed. Emily and I want to adopt Maddy and she told us this morning she'd like us to proceed."

"Awesome. Now you get to pay for college, a car when she turns eighteen, and oh—her wedding."

"Very funny. I am nothing but excited at the prospect. Don't worry about a wedding. No boy is getting near her unless he rivals Jesus Christ himself. How about you? Do you see a future with Megan? She's young enough to have kids."

"I'm taking it one step at a time. So far, so good. I would kinda like a few rug rats running around the house."

Henry pulled in front of the Aster Inn. "Operation nail Brody Wilkerson is now in motion." Pat followed him into the lobby. He wasn't sure what he was planning to do when he approached the desk.

"May I help you?" The clerk behind the counter adjusted his over-sized bow tie and the blazer he was swimming in.

"I hope so." He read the name tag. "Trevor, my buddy Brody Wilkerson, stayed here a few weeks ago. He called me and asked if I could swing by and pick up a duplicate bill. He needs it for reimbursement ASAP and he lost his copy. I'll be seeing him tomorrow."

Trevor, who looked as young as Maddy, said, "How do you spell his name?"

Henry spelled it out, surprised that the information would be handed over so freely. He reminded himself never to stay there if he had anything to hide.

"Here it is. I'll print it out."

Henry took the bill, thanked the clerk, and suggested eating in the restaurant next door. He and Pat waited for a table at the rustic, barn-styled restaurant.

"I'll bet Brody ate here. There's no other place to eat within miles."

Pat nodded. "When we sit down, let's have a look at the bill."

Henry and Pat were seated at a booth. Henry ordered a grilled chicken salad, and Pat ordered the meatloaf with mashed potatoes.

Henry pulled out the bill. "Well, he was here for two nights, just prior to the murder." He poured over the bill. "There are several charges. One is for a movie, ordered at 5 p.m., then room service ordered at 11:00."

"This place has room service?"

"It's Sugarbury Falls. You know the slogan: *we cater to our visitors*. What time did you place the murder?"

"Somewhere between six and midnight."

When the waitress set the food on the table, Henry said, "That was quick. My buddy, Brody was here a few weeks ago and raved about the service here. I wonder if you were his waitress?"

"I work six days a week, so chances are I was here."

Henry pulled up an internet photo on his phone. "Does he look familiar?"

She took the phone and enlarged the photo. "Yes, I remember him. He ate here a couple of times. Poor guy was very upset. I heard him on the phone with his girlfriend, begging her to let him come over."

"Did he go?" said Henry.

"No, at least not right away. He sulked over his meal, then I saw him at the bar when my shift ended at 10:00. He was sitting with someone—pretty, but older."

"Blonde hair?" said Henry, thinking about Danielle's blond hair spread on the floor underneath her.

"No, dark hair, almost black. I better get moving, the couple over at the next table is giving me a look."

Henry paid the bill, and once in the car, he discussed the information with Pat.

"How long would he need to drive there and back?"

"It doesn't matter. We don't know when the killer stuffed the chimney. It could have been days earlier."

"It had to have been the same day. It was chilly all week," said Henry. "I'll bet Kurt will know if Danielle used the fireplace the night before. He notices everything and is always taking that dog of his on walks. I think he uses dog walking as a cover for being nosy."

They finished lunch and hopped back into the Jeep. Pat checked his watch. "We have time to swing by Kurt's if you want."

Without hesitation, Henry agreed. "Can't hurt to try." He thought about what the waitress told him. A dark haired, older woman? The contenders for the cat commercial were in town then. Sheila was blond…Winnie? Was it possible? He pulled into Kurt's driveway behind a Ford Escape. "Looks like he's home. Let's go."

Kurt answered the door wearing a flannel shirt and Levis. "Is everything alright? Are Emily and Maddy okay?" He ushered them into the house.

"Yes, it's nothing like that. Pat and I were wondering if you happened to notice whether or not Danielle used the fireplace the night before she was murdered?"

"She used it every night since she moved in," said Kurt. "I'd already had to bring her more firewood and after dinner, Prancer and I always saw smoke coming out of the chimney. Why do you ask?"

"Trying to determine when the chimney was blocked. Must have been the same day as the murder. You didn't see anyone, did you?"

"I was in town most of the day. Had a doctor's appointment and errands to do, sorry."

"You helped quite a bit. We now know whoever blocked the chimney did it sometime during the day of the murder, not before."

"Did you ask the new girls over there if they saw anything?" He pointed to a neighboring cabin, on the other side of the rental.

"No, I hadn't realized anyone had moved in."

"Megan said she talked to the neighbors and they didn't see anything. I'm guessing she meant those neighbors," said Pat. "Hey, we'd better get back to the hospital. Thanks, Kurt."

Chapter 20

Henry pulled into an empty driveway, just beating the school bus. He waited at the front door for Maddy.

"Did you have a better day today? You look happier."

"I told my guidance counselor about the cat café and she thought it was a great idea. She even called the animal shelter while I was there and told them about it."

"I'll bet they loved it."

"They did and they were hoping we can get it up and running within the next couple of weeks. They try to clear out the shelter as much as possible before winter sets in so they have room for strays that are left to fend for themselves in the cold. They sponsor a free adoption week in the middle of October and suggested the opening of the café could coincide with it."

"We'd better get busy! Did you check on the necessary permits?"

"If the café itself is separate from the food prep area, we're good to go. I'm going to call a few pet stores and see if they'd be willing to donate litter boxes, scratching posts, cat toys..."

"Lots of garage sales and craft fairs this time of year. You might check them out. And I'll build another cat tree for you. Now that your bookshelf is done, I need another project." He heard the key in the front door.

Emily hung her sweater on the coat rack. "I can always find projects for you if you're desperate."

Maddy said, "He's volunteering to build a few cat trees for Coralee's Cozy Cat Café. My guidance counselor loved the idea and we want to get it up and running by the end of the month."

"That's great, Maddy. Is the room ready to go?"

"No, it still needs painting and furniture. I'd like to find an artist to paint a mural."

"I'll ask at the college. I'm proud of you. This project will really make a difference."

"I'm going to get my homework done now so I can work on the cat café after dinner." She scooped up Chester and went into her room.

Emily plopped down on the sofa next to Henry. "This could be a real turning point for her. By the way, I called a lawyer and he's sending me the paperwork we need to start the adoption rolling."

"Wouldn't it be nice if we had the adoption finalized before the holidays?"

"It'll be a whole new experience with Maddy. She can help us pick out the Christmas tree and help me bake cookies."

"Real cookies, right? None of those cardboard vegan ones."

"Real cookies—sugar and all."

"I went over to the Aster Inn today. The guy at the desk verified Brody was a guest at the time of the murder. Then I spoke to one of the waitresses. The night Danielle was murdered, she overheard Brody talking to his girlfriend and begging her to let him come over."

"So he *did* go over there."

"No, she says when her shift ended around ten, he was moping at the bar and talking to an older woman with dark hair."

"That fits Winnie's description, but she never mentioned seeing him in town before the day we ran into him at Coralee's. Why would she hide that?"

"You don't know it was her. And if he was calling Danielle that night trying to reconcile, why would he have blocked the chimney earlier that day? Charges for room service and a movie, plus being seen by the waitress, make it unlikely he went to the cabin the night of the murder."

Emily got up and fished her phone out of her purse. She tried calling Winnie, but got voicemail. "I left a message. Let's see if she gets back to me."

Emily changed her clothes and made a cup of coffee in her Keurig. She rummaged through the fridge trying to decide what to make for dinner while Henry researched cat tree designs on his laptop. "Henry, did you hear a knock?"

Henry closed his computer. "I'll get it. It's probably Kurt."

Two woman and a border collie were on the other side of the door. "Hi, I'm Abby and this is Rebecca." The dog whined. "Oh, and this is Milo. We met your wife earlier. We're your new neighbors."

"Henry Fox," he shook their hands. "Come on in. Emily's in the kitchen. Emily, we have visitors."

Emily dried her hands on her way to the living room. "Abby and Rebecca, I'm glad you stopped by."

Abby said, "Remember this morning when you asked if we'd seen anyone lurking around the cabin next door to us?"

"Do you remember something?"

Abby took a photo out of a manila envelope. "I was developing a roll of pictures I'd taken of the landscape and the lake. One of the pictures had the neighbor's cabin in the background. I noticed something. There's a ladder perched against the side of the cabin, and if you look closely, someone's hand is grabbing the rung. It's blurry, but I enlarged it and you can see it's definitely a gloved hand and the coat sleeve looks like some sort of plaid wool. I wish I'd gotten the face, but I was shooting the mountaintop on the horizon."

Emily held the photo up to her eye. "You're right! And this isn't the type of coat Kurt would ever wear. Henry, do you think it's Brody?"

Henry took the photo from Emily. "If you look carefully, you can see the shadow on the ground. What time was this taken?"

"Late afternoon. It's date stamped."

Emily said, "That's the day Danielle died! I'll bet this is the killer. Can we tell anything about the person from his shadow?"

Henry said, "I certainly can't."

Emily said, "Nancy's husband! He's an engineer. He designs bridges. I'll bet he can help us. Let me call her."

"Go for it."

Nancy answered on the first ring. "Nancy, is Byron home? We need his expertise as an engineer."

"Yeah, he just got home. What do you need?"

"One of our new neighbors happened to take a photo the day Danielle died. She captured the shadow of a person holding the ladder and we think it's probably the killer. We need someone to look at the shadow and determine whatever he can about the person's physique."

"Byron works with measurements all day long. I'm sure he can help. Come on over."

"Thanks, Nancy. You're the best." She relayed the conversation to Henry and the girls.

"I hope it helps," said Abby.

"I'm sure it will," said Emily. "Thank you so much for coming over with it. I'd love it if you and Rebecca could come over for dinner one night."

"Sounds great, but I have to warn you, Rebecca's a staunch vegetarian."

Emily thought it couldn't get more perfect. Maddy would love her. "So is my daughter. And she's gotten me on the bandwagon as well."

"I've got some excellent recipes to share," said Rebecca. "We look forward to it."

After the girls left, Emily ran into Maddy's room. "Hey, our new neighbor is a vegetarian. And they have the most adorable Border Collie. I think you'll like them."

"Okay."

Emily imagined the unspoken *and so what* and thought she'd once again come on too enthusiastically, but was getting tired of monitoring her conversations with Maddy. "Henry and I are running over to Nancy's. Do you want to come and visit with Brooke?"

"No, I've got a ton of homework, and I want to do some more work on the café, like I said."

"I just had a thought. One of our new neighbors is a photographer. Maybe she'd be willing to help with the advertising. She could take photos as the cafe is being put together, and I could write up a series to go in the local paper following its progress."

"That sounds like a great idea."

Emily hid a smile as she left the room. She grabbed her coat, and she and Henry hopped into the Jeep.

"I hope Byron can help us. I'd love to hand over a description as well as the photo to the police."

"Our new neighbors seem pleasant. They didn't have to go the extra mile and blow up the picture."

"I know." Her phone vibrated. "It's Winnie."

"Get it. Frankly, I'm surprised she called you back."

"Winnie, thanks for returning my call. No, the police haven't arrested anyone yet. We found out that Brody was in town at the time of the murder."

"Really?"

"Be honest, Winnie. You already knew that. A waitress at the Aster Inn saw you talking to Brody."

"She saw *me*? I don't think so. Why would I be talking to Brody after what he did to my mother?"

"If you want to help nail the killer, you have to tell the truth."

Winnie was silent. Emily thought she'd lost the connection. "Emily, I'll tell you the truth. I ran into him at the mini-mart and followed him to his hotel. That evening, I drove back there to confront him about his part in my mother's death. He'd been drinking and had no problem telling me the truth. He knew Splash Panels had a structural problem, but Wallace Hartman was pressuring him to go ahead with it. The money was tempting as well. He said he was sorry, but it was a little too late for that."

"Did he offer to come clean?"

"Not at all."

"Why didn't you tell the police you'd seen him? He swore he hadn't come to Sugarbury Falls until after Danielle's death."

"I didn't want to give him an alibi. I didn't know the details of Danielle's death, and I figured if I said I was with him the night she was murdered, he'd get off the hook. I'd still like to see him rot in jail, but I'll call the detectives in the morning and tell them what I just told you."

"Okay, Winnie. And I firmly believe in karma. In the end, Brody will get his due."

"Emily, one more thing. Brody said something about 'the three of them equally taking the blame'. I figure he and Hartman are two, but I don't know who he meant by the third. Only thought is maybe he was talking about the owner of Splash Panels."

"Do you have any names in mind?"

"At the trial, the owner of Splash Panels went by 'said owner.' They were careful not to name him, even though the case at that trial was against Splash Panels and not Nature's Vista."

"Thanks, Winnie. You need to tell the detectives everything you told me." She put the phone back in her purse. "I don't think Brody did it. Winnie thinks there was a third party involved with Hartman and Brody, maybe an investor, or the mysterious owner of Splash Panels."

"The police can get that information, I think." Henry pulled up to a brick farmhouse with white trim. The mailbox at the end of the driveway read *The Pattersons.*

"Come on in," said Nancy. "Byron's in the kitchen." She shouted, "Byron, they're here."

Byron Patterson, in an oversized cardigan, looked like a college professor. Emily loved his English accent. Nancy met him when she spent a semester abroad in Wales during her junior year at Bryn Mawr and after graduation, he moved to the states to be with her.

"Nancy says you need my expertise."

Emily took the photo out of her purse. "Can you calculate the man's size by the angle of the shadow?"

Byron took the picture and adjusted his glasses. "I believe so. Give me a few minutes." Byron took out some measuring tools that Emily couldn't identify and plugged numbers into his laptop. She held her breath, hoping he had enough to work with.

Byron looked up from the table. "I'd say the man was around five ten give or take. Under six feet for sure. He appears to have a bit of a stomach, too."

"Henry said, "You can tell all that from a shadow?"

"All in a day's work. Looks like this was taken late in the day."

"It was," said Henry. "You should sign on as a police consultant."

Byron chuckled. "Maybe when I retire I'll consider it."

Nancy said, "I just made a pot of coffee, and there's apple pie in the fridge. Come, sit down."

Brooke came into the kitchen. "I heard you say apple pie. Oh, hello Mr. and Mrs. Fox. Is Maddy here, too?"

"No," said Emily. "She had a lot of homework. I hate to ask, but does Maddy seem okay at school? Is she making any friends?"

"She keeps to herself, but the last few days, she's not scowling as much."

Nancy served the pie. "Give her time. This is all new to her."

Emily hoped she was right. The cat café project might be the thing that makes her feel like part of the community. That, and officially becoming a member of the Fox family.

Chapter 21

Saturday morning, Emily went on an early run, then sat down to work on her new book. Mair still lived in the same place she did when Nathan disappeared. Maybe if she got a good look at the house and property she'd come up with some ideas as to where the body could be hidden. She pulled up the five acres of property on Google Maps. According to Mair's ex-husband, he wanted to sell the place in the divorce, but she refused. How could you live in a place where you lost your only child like that? She herself would want to move as far away from the horror of that day as possible. Like her own mother did, after her sister...

Henry came in from a morning bike ride. "Hard at work on the new book?"

"Yep. I'm wondering where Mair dumped her son's body. She couldn't have gone far, since her husband said the gas needle hadn't moved."

"Didn't the police check the car for evidence?"

"They found nothing, but Nathan's father said the area rug was missing. She could have wrapped him in it."

"You think she was able to wrap her lifeless son in a rug and carry him to the car all by herself?"

"Nathan's father thinks she poisoned him. Problem is, Nathan wouldn't go outside without his shoes. And the police did a thorough search of the property after he disappeared."

"What are you thinking? Was there a pond on the property, or a lake?"

"Supposedly they sent divers into the lake and they found nothing. I'd like to see that property for myself. Mair left campus early yesterday. I overheard her say she was going to New York for the weekend."

"And you want to go scout it out, right?"

"Couldn't hurt. Want to come?"

"Sure, after I take a shower. I'm going over to the inn this afternoon to help paint the new cat room."

Emily closed her laptop and grabbed the adoption forms from her nightstand. She and Henry had filled them out the previous night, and she was hoping to get them in the mail today. There was space for additional information and she wondered if it would speed thinks along if Maddy stated her desire to proceed with filing the paperwork. She went downstairs to Maddy's room.

"Maddy, Henry and I are going to do some research for my book. On the way, I thought we'd drop these forms in the mail. Would you like to make a statement before I seal it up?"

Maddy took her time reading through them. Then she grabbed a pen off her desk. "I'm writing that my guardian has been taking excellent care of me since my mother's death and I'd like nothing more than to join the Fox family." She signed it with a flourish.

For a moment, Emily wondered if she was being sarcastic, but took the plunge. She hugged Maddy, perhaps a little too tightly. "I'm so happy you want to be with us."

Maddy didn't pull away, but instead hugged back. "Me, too."

Henry, hair wet from his shower, said, "Can I join in?" In a Hallmark movie moment, all three embraced. "Maddy, do you want to come for a ride with us? Mo...Emily wants to scout out the scene of the crime for her new book." He couldn't believe he almost referred to Emily as mom. Nothing like scaring Maddy away.

"Sure. As long as we're back in time to paint."

It was a beautiful, fall day. The leaves contrasted radiantly against the clear blue sky, making for an idyllic ride through the country. On the way to Oakbridge, they passed a makeshift apple cider stand fashioned from a barrel, and pickup trucks selling tomatoes and other produce out of wooden crates. Entering the town, they passed under an iron arch which read *Welcome to Historic Oakbridge.*

"We've arrived," said Henry. "Keep your seat belts fastened." The main street was two blocks long, lined with wrought iron hanging lanterns and covered in large cobblestones that made Maddy bob up and down in the back seat.

"Look, they have their own history museum," said Emily, pointing out her window.

Henry said, "My parents brought me to that museum one summer. This town's been here since before Vermont officially became a state."

"If we follow this road and take the first right, her house will be about a mile in."

Henry followed Emily's instructions, turning onto a dirt road, lightly covered with gravel. He pulled in front of a two story, white, wooden farmhouse with a wrap-around porch. "Here we are."

"It looks kinda like The Outside Inn, only older," said Maddy.

They parked in the dirt driveway and walked up to the house. The porch was completely empty. Emily knew if she lived here, she'd have set out a few wooden rockers, and maybe a two-person swing. Then again, Mair was the antithesis of cozy. God forbid her house should look inviting.

"There's a brass plate on the wall," said Maddy. She ran her hand across it. "This is officially a historic building." She tried the door. "It's locked."

"Did you think it wouldn't be?" asked Emily.

"Isn't everybody uber-trusting in these small towns?" Maddy peeked in the window. "Did they check under the porch?"

"Probably one of the first places they looked." Henry peeked through the wooden grate under the porch. "If a dead body was under there, the smell would have tipped them off pretty quickly."

Emily made her way around the back of the house. "Look, they have one of those cellars you can get to from outside." She stepped on the cement and tugged at the handles of the inclined, wooden doors.

Henry came around back. "They had to have checked there."

"Look," said Maddy. She pointed to a tire hanging from a tree.

"The best kind of swing," said Henry. "We had one at our cabin when I was growing up. It hung from the big oak tree in the back yard." He wondered if Maddy was too old to enjoy it if he rigged one up at home.

Emily tried the back door. "Everything's locked. Why don't we explore the rest of the property?" She should have known Mair would have kept everything locked up tight.

"It's a lot to explore on foot. I suggest we drive," said Henry. "Come on."

Emily and Maddy got into the Jeep. Henry drove slowly around the fir tree-lined perimeter of the property. They passed what once must have been a barn, but was now a concrete foundation with rotting wood piled on top. They parked and took a look.

"Maybe he's in there," said Maddy.

"She couldn't have buried the body so quickly, and the police searched the whole property as soon as Nathan went missing," said Emily. She walked around the foundation and spotted a small, shack-like structure. "I'll bet that used to be servant's quarters."

"You mean slaves?" said Maddy.

Henry, anxious to impart his historical knowledge on Maddy, said, "You know, Vermont was the first state to outlaw slavery." They walked toward the building and Henry rubbed the dirty window with the sleeve of his jacket. "Just one big room. I don't see a body in there."

Maddy pointed behind the shack. "What's that?"

"An outhouse," said Henry. "Did you say you needed the bathroom?"

Maddy groaned. "Are we heading back soon? I don't want to be late for the painting party."

"I guess we're not going to find much. The police searched thoroughly. If she hid the body on the grounds, it'd have to be some secret cave or something," said Emily. She wasn't sure what she'd expected to find, but nevertheless felt disappointed that their search left them empty handed. "I'm ready to go."

As they came nearer to the house, they spotted a car pulling into Mair's driveway. "Henry, park here, behind this tree. That looks like Mair's car. She was supposed to be away this weekend."

A dark haired woman got out of the passenger's side. The driver walked around and gave her a long, drawn out kiss.

Emily said, "Who's she with?"

"We're too far away to see. Open the glove compartment. There are binoculars in there."

"Binoculars?" said Maddy. "Emily, how much do you know about this husband of yours?"

"It's for bird watching," said Henry. "Get your mind out of the gutter, child."

Emily grabbed the binoculars. "It's definitely Mair and some man I've never seen before. Maddy, can you get a photo with your phone?"

"Let me take it through the binoculars."

Emily never knew you could do such a thing. Henry was impressed that Maddy came up with the idea.

"Got it. They're going inside now."

After the front door closed, Henry started up the Jeep and headed back to Sugarbury Falls. Emily wondered if maybe the trip wasn't quite as fruitless as she'd thought.

Chapter 22

When they arrived at Coralee's, the painting party was in full swing. Emily stepped onto the white, tarp protected floor and drank in the smell of fresh paint. Fresh paint evoked memories of the past as well as anticipation of the future—moving into her brand new childhood home when she was in fifth grade, a bedroom transformed into her sister's nursery, a freshly painted bookcase stenciled with Maddy's name...

Henry looked up at Franklin the handyman, and Coralee's son, Noah, perched on ladders, rolling paint across the ceiling. A splatter of white paint narrowly missed his shoulder. New neighbors Abby and Rebecca, in matching overalls, covered the moldings and door handle with blue tape.

Brooke said, "Hi, Maddy. This is going to look great!" She and her mom, Nancy, mixed paint with wooden spatulas. Brooke held the spatula, dripping green paint over the can. "Don't you love this color? Looks like a peaceful park or something."

Maddy said, "I can't believe you all showed up to help!"

Brooke said, "I'll get service hours for this, which is good, since I haven't yet come up with a project of my own."

Finished taping the door handle, Rebecca stood up and stretched her back. "Abby's an artist as well as a photographer. She volunteered to paint that mural you talked about after the initial painting is done. Wait till you see."

"I can help her," said Brooke. "I've been painting since I was in preschool."

Emily felt her heart warmed by the outpouring of support. Everything was falling into place. Maddy was adjusting to school, and although Emily understood she would always carry the pain of her mother's loss, she was thrilled to see her awakening out of her depression thanks to the cat café.

Nancy handed her a brush. "Why don't we start here." Brooke lugged the can of paint closer to the wall.

"Nance, we just took a ride over to Mair's place."

"I thought she was out of town?"

"I thought so, too. I wanted to get a look at the property. I thought it might help my writing. Anyhow, Mair pulled up with an older man. From their body language, I take it they're romantically involved, though it's hard to imagine anyone falling for her. Maddy took a picture on her phone." She called Maddy over. "Can you show Nancy the picture you took outside Mair's house?"

Maddy pulled her phone out of her back pocket. "Here you go."

Nancy enlarged the photo with her fingers. "I've never seen him before. Maybe she worked with him at her old school. I have a friend who works at that school. Want me to ask?"

"Sure."

"Send me the picture."

Coralee carried in a tray of cookies and a pitcher of warm apple cider. "Food to keep you going. Help yourselves." The sweet smell of cinnamon and spice was irresistible, and the tray was empty within minutes.

As the day progressed, the cat café came to life. The walls were done, and Franklin and Noah brought in the cat condo they'd been building. It reached floor to ceiling, with three balconies and a built in scratching post. Maddy and Brooke painted chairs that Coralee had pulled out of storage.

"I'm building a couple of coffee tables. I can knock them off this week," said Henry.

Maddy looked around. "Do you think we can be ready to open next weekend?"

Abby wiped her hands on her overalls. "I'll start on the mural tomorrow, and I've been taking photos all day. Your mom says she has connections with the local paper." She looked at Emily.

Not bothering to correct the assumption she was Maddy's mom, Emily said, "I'll write up a press release and they can run it in the local section mid-week."

It was well past dinner time, when Abby and Rebecca left. The room had been thoroughly transformed. Franklin and Noah volunteered to add the second coat of paint the next day.

Emily was covering the paint cans when Nancy brought over her phone. "I sent the picture to my friend and she got back to me already. Guess what? The man Mair was with is the married principal at the school where Mair worked when she got into all that trouble falsely accusing her colleagues. No wonder she wasn't immediately fired."

"*Married* Principal, huh? I wonder how long it has been going on."

"My friend has worked there her whole career. She says the gossip mill had them together before her son's disappearance. In fact, there were rumors Mair was trying to send her son away to an institution to clear the way for her to divorce Nathan's father and get together with the boss."

"Interesting. What if Mair didn't carry her son's body all by herself? What if she had help in the form of a strong, muscular lover? And suppose that helper brought his own car and carted the boy far away where he'd never be found?"

"Emily, I think this book you're writing just got ever more intriguing. I'll bet you're on to something."

"We're going to grab something to eat. Want to join us?"

"I'd love to, but Byron's got dinner in the oven. Keep me posted. I'll see you Monday."

Emily washed her hands and ran a brush through her hair before heading into the dining room. She wiped a smudge of paint off Maddy's face.

"I've worked up an appetite, how about my girls?" said Henry.

"Starving," said Emily. Maddy nodded her head.

The dining room had mostly cleared out given the late hour. When they were seated, Pat and Megan came over.

"Romantic dinner for two?" said Henry.

"Yep. And now it's off to see a late movie. Sorry I couldn't help out today. I just got off work a little while ago. So did Megan."

Megan, looking adorable in a short black dress, said, "I was going to call you. We found out the name of the third wheel. It's an investor who heavily funded both Splash Panels and the Nature's Vista franchise Officially, he owns Splash Panels."

"Really? Does he fit the description we got from Byron Patterson?"

"Not that the description we have from measuring a shadow is the gold standard, but yes, it could be the same person."

Emily leaned in. "Do you know whether or not he was in Sugarbury Falls the night Danielle was murdered?"

"We're working on it. Megan looked at her watch. Pat, we have to get going if we want to make the movie."

Pat pulled out Megan's chair. "Enjoy. I'm free next weekend to help out with the café, Maddy."

"Thanks. We're hoping to have it up and running very soon."

Emily didn't open the menu. On the way into the dining room, she noticed mushroom ragout on the chalkboard listing the specials and her mind was made up. Maddy ordered a veggie burger with sweet potato fries, while Henry splurged on the chicken pot pie.

"Do you think Pat is going to wind up marrying Megan?" asked Emily.

"Who knows. For now, they're enjoying each other's company."

Maddy picked apart one of the yeasty rolls in the basket. "I want to have our grand opening next weekend. Emily, you said you'd write the article you were talking about with Abby's photos. I'm going to ask Coralee who prints her menus and business flyers."

Henry said, "I know an on-line printing company that can make them for you overnight, for an extra fee. Tell me what you want and I'll take care of it for you."

"Emily, do you have a pen in your purse?"

"Here you go. And here's the back of a flyer that was stuck under my windshield if you need paper."

Maddy sketched out her ideas. "If we wait till the next weekend, it will be Halloween and there will be too much competition for our opening. If we wait longer, it's going to be way too cold for the outdoor strays."

Coralee placed the food on the table. "What's that? Your first advertising?"

"Yep. We want to have the grand opening next weekend. Are we being too ambitious?"

"Not at all. I mentioned it to some of our guests and everyone is in love with the idea. Enjoy your dinners."

After more planning, and a satisfying dinner, they piled into the Jeep for the short ride home. Emily could barely keep her eyes open, and in the rearview mirror, saw Maddy curled up on the back seat. She'd tell all her students and colleagues at work about the café, and knew Coralee would also get the word out. She shuddered with excitement imagining Maddy being interviewed by the local news, holding shelter cats in her arms while she talked. She closed her eyes, rocked by the motion of the car, she leaned her head against the slightly open car window and relaxed, the cool night air brushing her face.

"Home, sweet home," announced Henry. Maddy stirred from the back seat.

As they approached the front door, Emily felt a chill. The front door was scratched around the knob, and the wood around the door jamb was splintered. "Henry!"

"Take Maddy and wait in the Jeep. Call 911. Go."

Henry carefully observed the front walk and worked his way around to the back of the house. His heart skipped a beat. Maddy's window had been smashed with a rock; shards of glass littered the grass outside the sill. He ran back to his car. "Someone broke in and for all we know may still be inside."

Chapter 23

The police arrived within minutes. Shortly after the squad car arrived, Detective Megan O'Leary, still wearing the black dress she'd worn earlier at dinner, stepped out of Pat's car and followed him to the door.

"Hey, buddy, what's going on? Is anybody hurt? Megan and I were at the movies when she got the message."

"We're okay. We got home and noticed the lock had been fooled with. Then we found Maddy's bedroom window smashed."

"Was anything taken?" asked Megan.

"We didn't go inside. We didn't know if the perpetrator was still in there."

Megan said, "Good thinking. I see Emily is already giving a statement."

A uniformed officer was taking to Emily and Maddy. Another came from around the corner of the house. "Coast is clear. There are tire tracks on the grass and the rock used to smash the glass is inside the room. Any idea as to who did this?"

"Emily thinks she was followed the other day. We're the ones who discovered Danielle LaPierre's body last month, along with our neighbor, Kurt. We've kind of gotten drawn into amateur investigating. Maybe it's related."

"Come in with me and let's see if anything was taken. It's your daughter's room, right? She should come, too."

Henry walked over to Emily and Maddy, who were still talking to the other officer.

"Maddy, come inside with me. The officer wants us to see if anything's missing."

Maddy followed him into the house. The sheets and comforter were heaped on the floor, and her mattress was half-way off the bedframe. Drawers were open and clothing had been thrown onto the floor. She wiped her moist eyes with her sleeve.

"Who would do this to me? It's not like I had money or jewels hidden in here!"

"Thank God we weren't here when it happened," said Henry. "Until this person is caught, we're not letting you out of our sight." He hugged Maddy close. "I know it's a mess, but do you notice anything missing right off the bat?"

Maddy looked around. "My laptop! And it has all my stuff for the cat café on it."

"Don't worry," said Henry. "It's all backed up on the cloud. You haven't lost it."

Henry checked the living room and the loft master bedroom, where Chester hid under the bed. "Nothing was taken as far as I can see. Doesn't look like he even came upstairs. Emily's laptop is sitting right on her desk and she has some expensive jewelry sitting on top of her dresser. I tell her all the time not to leave it lying around."

The officer took notes while Henry spoke. "We'll get some pictures and send the crime guys over to look for prints and get a mold of the tire tracks. Do you have a place to spend the night?"

Henry said, "I'm sure we can get a room at the Outside Inn for the night. Where's Emily and Detective O'Leary?"

The officer checked his phone. "They went over to your neighbor's to see if he witnessed anything."

Maddy said, "I'm getting Chester. I don't want him to stay here without us."

After gathering a few things, Maddy and Emily followed Henry to the Jeep. Emily was glad she'd grabbed a jacket for both herself and Maddy. The roads were deserted, and in no time at all, they pulled up to the familiar inn which was practically a second home. Coralee's son, Noah, on nightshift behind the front desk, took off his headphones when he saw them enter.

"Weren't you just here?"

Henry explained what had happened. "I hope you've got a couple of rooms for us. I know it's the height of tourist season."

Noah scrolled through the computer. "Hmm, nothing. Wait, we've got two rooms left if you don't mind some half painted walls and bare floors. We're in the middle of renovating the first floor rooms. Otherwise, we're booked solid this weekend. Mom won't charge you."

"Thanks, Noah." Emily took the key, anxious to crawl into bed. After getting Maddy settled in her room, she and Henry collapsed on top of the four poster bed next door.

"I'm going to grab a quick shower," said Henry. He pried himself off the comforter and feeling like he was eighty years old, dragged his tired bones to the bathroom.

Emily closed her eyes for a few minutes, then unpacked her nightgown and robe. Clearing the bed, she grabbed a hanger and put her jacket in the closet. As soon as she closed the closet door, she heard a crash. The clothing bar had pulled out of the wall and ripped a hole into the side of the closet. Coralee had made the decision to renovate just in the nick of time. The inn dated back to the 1700's and was overdue for repairs.

She pushed away the chunks of plaster. When she leaned her hand on the interior wall, it caved in as though it was made of wet cardboard. Something looked strange. She pulled the chain on the single light bulb above her head and now saw that the wall was completely damp. Looking up, she found the source—a leak coming from the top of the closet, dripping down its side wall.

"What are you doing in the closet?" asked Henry. He was wrapped in a fluffy towel, shivering.

"The clothing bar collapsed. There's a leak in here." She ran her hand along the damp wall, causing it to crumble like wet plaster. Her hand poked through the wall with no effort at all.

She pulled it apart with her hands. "Henry, look!"

Henry, pulling his towel tighter, bent down and peeked in. "What's that?"

"It looks like a secret room of some sort." She kicked the remainder of the wall with her foot. "I'm going exploring." She stepped over the crumbled plaster. "Henry, there's a metal trunk of some sort." She tugged at it, trying not to break a fingernail. After a bit of persistence, she was able to open the dusty lid.

"What did you find?" Henry squeezed into the small room next to his wife.

"Some blankets, an oil lantern, and tin cans. I think there's food inside. I wonder if Coralee knows about this?"

"If she did, I'm sure she'd have cleaned it out. If the wall hadn't collapsed, it'd still be hidden. Who'd think to go looking for a secret room? I'm freezing. We'll clue her in at breakfast."

Emily was about to follow Henry back into their room, when she heard a creak. She stomped her foot and heard it again. "Wait, Henry."

"What's wrong?"

"I think there's a trap door or something." She bent down and felt the rotting floor. "Here!"

Henry helped her pull up the boards. "You're right!" He tugged at it and it creaked open. "There' a ladder! It's too dark, we can't go down there."

"I'm going to get Noah. I'm sure he has a flashlight. Put on some clothes."

Emily ran out to the lobby. "Noah." He didn't flinch. Coming closer, she saw he had his earphones in and shouted, "Noah!"

Noah jumped. "What's wrong? Do you need towels or something?"

"No, we need a flashlight. Henry and I discovered a secret passage!"

"A what?"

"Do you have a flashlight or not?"

"Yeah." He pulled one from under the desk. "We keep one right here in case the electricity goes out." He followed her back to the room, where Henry was busy clearing away more plaster.

Henry grabbed the flashlight and illuminated the trap door, then shone the beam into the opening. "I wouldn't want to try that ladder. Looks well-rotted."

"I gotcha," said Noah, grabbing the flashlight from Henry. "It's not deep at all." He stepped down the rungs. "It looks like a tunnel. If I'm not back in a few…"

Emily shouted, "Are you crazy? Get back here!" He was already out of sight. Emily considered dialing 911, but Henry calmed her down.

"Give him five minutes. It's probably a root cellar, where they kept vegetables stored for the winter months."

Emily squirmed, thinking of the possible consequences. If anything happened to Noah, Coralee would never forgive her for summoning her foolish son in the middle of the night and putting him in harm's way. She stared at her watch. "Henry, we have to get help."

Henry was about to agree, when they heard a knock. He flung open the door. "Noah! We were just about to call the police."

"You're full of mud. What did you find?" asked Emily.

"It's a tunnel. I'm sure it was part of the original building. It leads outside behind the barn."

"Why on earth did they need a secret tunnel?" said Emily.

Henry cleared his throat. "I think I know. Remember that museum in Oakbridge we passed? I told you how my parents were history buffs. I think it was used to hide fugitive slaves. Vermont was anti-slavery from the start."

"My mom is going to love this!" said Noah.

Chapter 24

Snuggled under the down comforter, Henry and Emily woke up when Maddy knocked on the door, Chester cradled in her arms. Emily, too tired to move, was glad that Maddy had slept through round two of last night's excitement.

"Are we staying here for brunch?" said Maddy.

"Of course." Emily swung her feet over the side of the bed. Looking at the clock on the nightstand, she was surprised she'd slept this late. It was nearly noon. "I'll jump into the shower and be ready shortly. Henry can fill you in on what we discovered last night."

Henry told Maddy what they'd found.

"I wanna see."

"You can peek through the closet wall, but don't go into the damp basement. I think I saw spiders."

The mention of spiders dissuaded Maddy. She peeked in the closet, then plopped on the bed and played with her phone while they waited for Emily.

"I'm hungry, how about you two?" asked Emily, coming out of the shower.

"Starved," said Maddy. Henry agreed.

As soon as they opened their door, they could smell the aroma of bacon and pumpkin pancakes. Every meal was an event at the inn, but Sunday Brunch was the academy awards. The dining room was packed, and they had to wait for a table.

Coralee ran up to them immediately, bubbling about the historic finding right here on her own property. "I'm going to get the historic society to put up another plaque. Maybe they'll put a model of the inn in that museum over in Oakbridge. Just think, my very own inn was once used to help slaves escape to freedom. Gives me chills thinking about it."

"You could start giving tours. You'd make some nice extra change," said Henry. "Better yet, you could do nighttime ghost tours."

Coralee wiped her hands on her apron. "Like I don't have enough to keep me busy." Max came from behind the front desk, nuzzling against Maddy's legs. "Max has made himself quite at home here. The guests love him."

Maddy said, "I can't wait until the grand opening of Coralee's Cozy Cat Café next weekend."

Megan and Pat came into the lobby.

"Don't you ever eat at home?" said Henry.

"Look who's talking," said Pat. "I hear the food's good and that they have this cool cat café."

Emily hadn't seen Pat look this good since his wife's death. The worry lines around his mouth had faded, and he looked ten years younger sporting an oversized Patriot's sweatshirt that matched the one Megan wore.

Maddy smiled. "By this time next week that'll be true."

"Have you recovered from last night?" said Megan.

"Barely. We had some more excitement after we got to the inn last night. If you join us for brunch, we can fill you in."

Henry said, "How long until we know if the prowler left behind any evidence?"

"The guys were at it into the wee hours of this morning. They found a cigarette butt on your lawn last night and were able to pick up fingerprints, though elsewhere, it seems he wore gloves."

"Really?" said Emily, surprised at the speed at which the police department worked. "Was it a match for the ones you found on the fuse box outside of Danielle's cabin? Or did they match anything in the system?"

"They matched the ones found at Danielle's. Neither set belongs to Brody, or to Winnie, for that matter."

"How about Hartman?" said Emily.

"Hartman is away at a friend's funeral in Atlanta. He gave the eulogy yesterday afternoon. It wasn't him. With those three eliminated, the only lead left is the investor working with Hartman and Brody. Detective Ron is checking into finding out his identity."

The waitress offered them menus, but they declined in favor of the spectacular buffet. Emily loaded her plate with veggie quiche and Belgian waffles topped with cinnamon apples. She wasn't used to eating so late and felt light-headed.

"How's school going?" asked Megan.

Emily cringed thinking about her new colleague and the additional stress she'd brought to St. Edwards. "Classes are good, but I have Lucifer herself as my new chair. I have no doubt she killed that son of hers. Why on earth hasn't she been arrested?"

"You do know her father was the police chief over in Oakbridge, right? Mysteriously, no evidence linked her to the crime, and due to the father's insistence, the ball was dropped way too prematurely."

"Hopefully my new book will reignite interest in the case. Maybe I'll even solve the mystery while doing my research. We took a ride over there. The grounds are humongous. There are so many places a body could be hidden."

"They claim to have run a thorough search, but I wasn't there. My first thought was that he fell into the lake on the property, but I do know one of the divers they sent and he was convinced the boy wasn't in there." She turned to Maddy. "And how's school going for you?"

Emily realized the question was directed at Maddy in the first place and felt her face turning red.

"It's going better than it was. I still don't have any friends, but I don't care anymore."

Emily wanted to cry whenever Maddy said something like that. She looked at Henry and saw the hurt in his eyes. She knew he couldn't stand not being able to fix whatever hurt Maddy, just like he ached whenever she herself was hurt. She loved that Henry was a fixer, believing every problem had a logical solution. She'd believed since she first met him that his desire to diagnose and solve problems was the primary reason he'd become a physician.

Breaking the awkward silence, Pat said, "I'm thinking a second helping of waffles is on the agenda." He had lost a lot of weight after his wife died, but was recently packing on a few pounds.

"Good thing you're wearing that roomy sweatshirt," said Henry. "Megan, you've got to get him to go easier on the bacon and sausage before it kills him."

Megan's phone vibrated. "It's Ron. I'll take it outside."

While Pat was at the buffet line, Maddy said, "Do you think those two are going to get married?"

"I hope so," said Emily. "He finally seems to be bouncing back to his old self. Megan has been good for him."

While Maddy finished her pancakes, and Emily sipped a second cup of coffee, the tables were clearing out. Emily looked at her watch. "Wow, I didn't realize how late it was. The weekend has flown by way too fast."

"You can say that again," said Maddy. "Can I stay home tomorrow? All the teachers post the work online anyway."

Henry put down his fork and pushed back into his chair. "I'm surprised you said that. Don't you realize how valuable a good education is? If you want to get into an ivy league school, you've got to stay on top of your game, and that means attending school."

Maddy gave him what Emily interpreted as a 'yes, Dad' nod. It was kind of sweet the way Henry had stepped into his role as a father so easily. She wished she felt as comfortable with the mother role. She truly loved Maddy, but sometimes she still felt awkward and unsure of herself in dealing with her.

Megan came back to the table on the heels of Pat, who carried a heaping plate of waffles and sausage links.

"Good news. Ron said they traced Brody and Hartman's third financial partner."

"That's great," said Emily. "Are they bringing him in for questioning?"

"It'd be voluntary, since we have nothing on him. He is the right height, though, according to the calculations Byron Patterson figured. Oh, and I left out the best part."

Emily and Henry both looked at her and waited through her dramatic pause.

Megan drew a slow breath. "Charles. Charles Wilkerson. Brody's father."

Chapter 25

The dark, colder mornings tempted Emily to stay in bed rather than lace up her running shoes and open the front door. She looked forward to the upcoming time change, though most everyone she knew rued the earlier evening darkness that came with it. She grabbed half a banana and a swig of juice, then off she went, giving herself kudos for self-discipline. She saw her breath in front of her like a chug from a locomotive as she progressed from a slow jog to an all-out run. Following the grass trail around the lake, she ran into a bundled up Abby, and Milo, sporting a Halloween-themed doggie sweater.

"I see you're up especially early today," said Emily. Now that she stopped, the trapped sweat beneath her running clothes chilled her.

"Milo needed to go out and Rebecca was fast asleep. She owes me one."

"Maddy was so happy to see you and Rebecca helping out Saturday. She's starting to find her place in this town, although I wish school was getting easier for her."

"It's only October. I bet by Christmas it'll be a whole different story. I'm going over to the inn later to start on the mural."

"Detective Megan thinks she identified the man in your photograph. You may have been the bridge to solving the murder."

"Happy to do my part, even if it was accidental. If you need help investigating on the sly, Rebecca is an expert. Her favorite part of her job involves digging up information through tracing online records."

"Really? I know the detectives are working on it, but if she can move things along even faster…"

"Let us know. Like I said, she loves playing private investigator." Milo pulled on the leash. "Better get going. See you at the grand opening if not sooner."

Emily continued her run. If Rebecca could find records of financial transactions between Brody, Hartman, and his father, would it lead to anything useable? She thought about what they knew. Danielle came to town for the cat commercial. She was a lawyer, and had defended her then boyfriend, Brody Wilkerson, who worked for Splash Panels. She won the case for him. Splash Panels, a newly patented air conditioning system, made its debut at Nature's Vista assisted living facility. A lot rode on it being a success. Hartman, head of the facility, was partners with Brody. A third partner, Charles Wilkerson, is Brody's father. Emily stopped and took a swig from her water bottle.

The air conditioning system failed, causing the death of Winnie's mother, amongst others. Because Splash Panels won the case, they had no financial responsibility toward the families of the residents. In fact, the residents turned over their assets to Nature's Vista when they moved in, and the families had no recourse in regaining those assets.

Winnie was furious. She happened to meet Brody at the cat audition outside Washington, D.C., and realized who he was. She blamed him for her mother's death. She had reason to murder Danielle when she realized it was Danielle who had defended Splash Panels.

Danielle found out Brody knew about the problem with Splash Panels and was possibly blackmailing him over it. Did Brody kill Danielle to keep her quiet? He lied about being in town at the time of her death.

Prints that matched the fuse box as well as a cigarette butt outside Maddy's window didn't belong to Brody, or to any criminal in the database. Abby's picture captured a shadow of a man climbing a ladder to the roof of Danielle's cabin, most likely to stuff it with clothing and insure the carbon monoxide would kill Danielle. Wallace Hartman had a stake in keeping things quiet, but he was attending a funeral at the time.

That left the third secret partner, Charles Wilkerson—Brody's father.

Emily walked the last part of her run, thinking while she cooled down. By the time she got home, Maddy had left for school, and Henry was walking out the door.

Henry kissed her. "Have a good day. Try not to get upset by Mair Rose, hard as it may be."

When Emily got to St. Edwards, she had a note—no—a reprimand waiting in her mailbox. She wanted to scream, and used every ounce of self-control to keep it in.

Nancy put her hand on her shoulder. "What's wrong?"

Through a clenched jaw, Emily said, "Nothing."

"Come on. I can read it all over your face."

"Follow me." She led Nancy to her office and closed the door. "This is from Mair. She says this is a formal warning regarding failure to meet instructional contact time." She slammed the paper into Nancy's hand.

"What! I didn't know there was a particular rule. Heck, I'm sure I'm breaking it too."

"She cites letting my students out early on three occasions, and had them sign it! Look at this! I wasn't even working on this day and she cites me for shortchanging the students. If she doesn't get thrown in jail soon, I'm serious about quitting. Henry's right. Who needs this?"

"What a witch! If we didn't need the money, I'd quit in a heartbeat. We have virtually nothing saved for Brooke's college education, and as it is we're praying for a huge scholarship to fall from the skies." She plopped down in the chair next to Emily's desk. "Let's see what dirt we can dig up. We have some time before class starts. Turn on your computer."

"I'm not sure what we're looking for. I wonder if her boyfriend, Mr. Principal, was ever questioned."

"You have to remember her father was in charge of the police department. I'm sure lots of things slipped through the cracks. Look him up."

"Which one?"

"Start with Mair's father."

Emily said, "Do you know his name?"

"Yeah, he was all over the news with the tough guy act after Nathan disappeared. It's Harold Kramer. If you'd lived here at the time, you'd remember, too. Came across as so insincere when he talked about finding his poor grandson on TV. I think there was a scandal going on some time after that forced him to retire. At least that's what the rumor mill said."

Emily googled his name and scrolled through the entries. "I'm not finding anything we can use. We need someone with more expertise to handle this. I have just the person, too."

"Who? Detective Megan?"

"No, our new neighbor, Rebecca. You met her at the painting party."

"Yes, she was very sweet."

"Her wife told me she had experience in private investigating and she's a computer whiz. I'll go by and talk to her after work."

"While you're at it, see what she can dig up on the principal."

"You got it. Come on, we don't want to short the students on instructional time."

*****

Henry beat both Maddy and Emily home. He was stuck on the idea of Brody's father being the third business partner, and the role he may have played in Danielle's death. He called Megan at work, but discovered she'd been called out of town on a family emergency. He hoped all was okay and would call Pat later to find out.

"Then, may I speak with Detective Wooster?"

After a few minutes, he was connected to Ron's office.

"Detective, it's Henry Fox. I was wondering if you were able to track down Brody Wilkerson's father? Megan told us he was a partner in the Splash Panels/Nature's Vista scandal."

"Megan told you all that?"

"We were the ones who found the body and we're helping however we can."

"Yes, we found him and we'll be following up when Detective O'Leary returns. You can check back with her."

Henry sensed Ron's uncomfortableness. After all, it wasn't standard practice for the police department to share information about an ongoing case with civilians. Having his best friend dating the lead detective certainly blurred the rules, but in this town, the big picture—finding a murderer—trumped the norm. "I wonder why he kept his partnership secret. Was it because he was afraid of being accused of nepotism?"

"No, I doubt that. They'd worked together before. I've got another call."

"Okay, I'll let you go."

Brody's father secretly helped his son by hiring him to install Splash Panels. Mair Rose's father was chief of police and covered up his grandson's murder to protect his daughter. It made Henry wonder how far he'd go to protect Maddy if push came to shove. Then he realized that the behavior of those fathers most probably *caused* their children's delinquency. He'd always been on the nurture side of the nurture vs. nature debate. He and Emily made it clear to Maddy what was and wasn't acceptable, and obviously, Fiona had done the same. He couldn't imagine being in that situation. Then, he thought about how sweet Coralee was and the rocky road she'd gone down with her son, Noah.

He was about to get on his computer, when he remembered his old medical school buddy who went into business in the D.C. area. They kept in touch a few times a year. Maybe he'd have a clue where to start. He scrolled through his contacts.

"Jack, yeah, it's me. Doing good. Emily's fine. Yes, it's great being a dad. Maddy's wonderful. I'm calling because I could use your help. I know you're in the business end of medicine. You still manage that private hospital in Fairfax, right?"

"Sure do. Hoping to retire in a couple of years so the wife and I can travel. What good's having money if you don't have the time to spend it?"

"I hear you. Do you know the name Charles Wilkerson?"

"Wilkerson…sure. He invested in a rehabilitation center some years back and was brought up on tax fraud charges. He was blackballed after that. No one around here would take his money."

"But if he had a partner, he could be the wind behind the scenes, right?"

"I suppose so. As long as his name wasn't associated with the funding, who'd care?"

"You heard about the whole Splash Panels/Nature's Vista fiasco, right?"

"Of course. Both dodged a bullet, winning the lawsuit and all. Had they lost, the responsible parties would have lost their shirts. Splash Panels had a damn good lawyer and once they won, Nature's Vista was off the hook, too. Gotta feel bad for the relatives of those residents who died like that."

"Tragic. Maybe things will be made right after all."

"What do you mean?"

"The lawyer who represented Splash Panels was murdered here in our town. She represented them as well as dated Brody Wilkerson, of Splash Panels."

"Wilkerson, like Charles Wilkerson?"

"His son. We found out Charles was a silent partner and may even be a killer."

"I thought you went to Vermont to relax and putter in your woodshop? Murder? Secret partners?"

"Never a dull moment. Keep in touch, buddy. If you ever get a free weekend, you and Carol ought to drive up for a long weekend. You still ski?"

"It's been a while, but yes, I still ski. I'll talk to Carol and maybe we can arrange something."

"Take care, buddy."

Chapter 26

Emily made a point of announcing to her class, "It's exactly 4:20, so it's time to leave." She was a little miffed that her students would sign the statements Mair required, however, upon further reflection, she understood they were likely not given much choice. Mair was intimidating just by her presence in the room. An evil aura radiated from her like a perverse sort of halo. Hungry, tired, but motivated to nail Mair, Emily headed to Abby and Rebecca's to see what Rebecca could dig up.

Before she could even knock, she heard Milo bark. Rebecca, wearing her Yale sweatshirt and fuzzy socks, answered the door.

"Hi, Emily. Abby said you might be stopping by. She's still at the inn working on the mural."

"Maddy really appreciates that."

"What can I help you with?"

"I was wondering what you can dig up on my boss, Mair Rose. Two years ago, her autistic son disappeared from their house while her husband was at work. Mair claims to have been asleep on the sofa at the time. The boy was never found."

"Mair Rose." Rebecca opened her computer and typed.

Emily's eyes scanned the homey cabin. On the end table, a candle nestled in a sea-glass jar radiated the aroma of warm vanilla. The walls were made of knotty wood, decorated with a hand-crafted quilt, a park scene fashioned from copper, and several framed photos which she assumed were Abby's work. On the oak coffee table, flip books of photos—the Cayman Islands, Alaska—and a wedding album. She flipped through the pages. Both girls were gorgeous in their wedding gowns. Abby's dress was lacy and romantic; Rebecca's, elegant satin with clean lines.

"Here it is, the whole story from the local paper. The community organized a giant search party and divers searched the lakes and ponds throughout the town. Says they found nothing."

Amazed at how quickly Rebecca found the information, Emily said, "Mair's father was Chief of Police in Oakbridge at the time. I think he covered things up because he knew his daughter was guilty."

"His own daughter killed her child? His grandson?"

"You'd have to meet Mair and you'd understand. The boy's father is convinced of her guilt, and she apparently had something going with her boss at the public high school. He may have helped her."

"Is her father still Chief of Police?"

"No, and from what I hear, his resignation was rather sudden. We weren't living here yet, but that's what my friend Nancy says."

"Give me a few more minutes. What's her father's name?"

"Harold Kramer."

Rebecca put on her glasses and typed away, laser focused on the job at hand. Milo inched his way over to Emily with a well-worn, rag toy in his mouth. He dropped it at Emily's feet and they engaged in a game of fetch while Rebecca worked.

"Here we go. Her father was accused of tampering with evidence associated with the Nathan Rose case. It was swept under the rug in exchange for his quiet resignation."

"How on earth did you find that so quickly?"

"I'm a pro," laughed Rebecca. "Evidence disappeared. According to officers working on the investigation, that included a baseball cap and an area rug. Also a bottle of grape juice."

"How do they know? Are the officers still working there?"

Rebecca called out some names, then searched. "One was transferred to San Diego, another took early retirement."

Emily's heart sank. "Figures."

"Wait, there's one more name. He was a rookie, new to the force. He's still there."

"I wonder if he'll talk to me."

"I'm sure he was scared to say anything, but now that Mair's father is gone, he may have changed his mind."

Emily wrote down the name. "You're a doll. Thank you. Hey, what smells so good?"

"It's my squash casserole. Should be ready soon, want to stay for dinner?"

"I'd love to, but Maddy and Henry are waiting for me. Thanks, again. I'll see you at the grand opening on Saturday, right?"

"Wouldn't miss it for anything. Milo can't wait."

Emily stammered, "I don't know if bringing a dog to a cat..."

"Relax. I was only kidding! Tell Maddy I said hello and that we can't wait till Saturday."

Emily drove home, wondering what the next plan of action should be. If she could drive out to Oakbridge again, perhaps she could speak to the rookie cop—if he was still working there. Rebecca was a terrific resource and she tucked away the many ways she could be useful in getting this book written. They should have also dug into Mair's connection to her old boss. One thing at a time.

When she walked in her front door, she saw Henry
and Maddy sitting on the sofa together, working a
Sudoku puzzle. She felt a warm glow just watching
them—her *family*.

"Hey, Em. Things run late at work?"

"No, I stopped by Rebecca and Abby's. Rebecca's a
whiz at internet investigating. Found out that evidence
went missing in the Nathan Rose case. The chief,
Mair's father, quietly resigned when he was implicated,
and two detectives working the case were transferred
across the country."

"So there's no one left on the force to interview?"

"There's one possibility. A rookie at the time was
kept on. I'm going to take a ride out to Oakbridge and
see if he's there and willing to talk to us."

"I'll come with you. When are you planning on
going?"

"Tomorrow? My class ends early."

Maddy looked up from the Sudoku. "Tomorrow's
Halloween. I'm not staying here alone!"

"Then you'll come with us," said Emily. "And while
we're there, maybe we can try exploring Mair's
property again. She left this afternoon for a
conference."

Henry said, "Want to hear my news? I did some
investigating of my own."

"Tell me," said Emily.

"Called an old med school buddy who lives in
Fairfax. He told me Charles Wilkerson was involved in
fraud and tax evasion before he was ever involved with
Splash Panels. He had invested in a rehabilitation
center. His reputation was ruined after that, which
explains why he'd have wanted to keep his name out of
the Splash Panels deal."

Maddy said, "Leave it to me to wind up having Miss
Marple and Hercule Poirot as parents."

Emily's heart stopped. She glanced at Henry, whose face showed he'd registered Maddy's comment as well. *As parents.* Why did she feel like she wanted to dance on the ceiling? For all the intellectualizing she'd done, for all the pros and cons lists she'd made, her physical reaction to those words said it all. She had a daughter and felt like she'd won the lottery.

Chapter 27

After school, Emily, Henry, and Maddy headed to Oakbridge. It was late afternoon, and they passed trick or treaters in pint-sized costumes. The sun was going down behind the mountains and some of the children wore glow sticks around their necks to make themselves more visible to passing vehicles. When Emily was a kid, her mother insisted she and her sister carry flashlights for the same reason.

"What did you dress up as when you were little?" asked Emily. For the first time, she felt maybe she'd missed out on something by not holding her child's hand, knocking on doors, and begging for candy.

"Mom made some great costumes. One year I was the Little Mermaid. Mom covered the bottom half of the costume with green glitter and we found glitter in the house for months. She said glitter was on the banned list when it came time to shop for the prom or my wedding."

Henry cleared his throat. "One year I dressed up like Gene Simmons from Kiss."

"What's that?" asked Maddy. "Some old movie?"

"What! You never heard of Kiss? They were the greatest heavy metal band ever. I covered my face with black and white theater makeup and carried a cardboard guitar." He belted out a guitar lick, making Maddy and Emily rush to cover their ears.

By the time they pulled into the Oakridge police station, the sun had set.

"What's the name of this officer we're looking for?' said Henry.

"Rebecca said it's Jay Hart. According to her, he works evenings and should be there."

When they walked into the police station, it was nearly deserted. A plastic Jack-o'-lantern on the counter brimmed with fun-sized Twix and Snickers. Henry grabbed a handful and slipped one to Maddy.

"Can I help you?" said a handsome, young officer. Emily read the name on his uniform. Jay Hart.

"I hope so," said Emily. "My name is Emily Fox. I'm a writer and we live over in Sugarbury Falls. I'm working on a true crime book about the Nathan Rose case and I understand you were on the force at the time."

Jay Hart looked at the floor and mumbled. "Yes. We consider that a cold case."

Emily said, "I'm just trying to verify some basic facts. I won't use your name if you'd rather I didn't. A boy has been missing nearly two years and his father is heartsick wondering if he might still be alive. At the very least, he should have the chance to bury his son properly." She doubted he was old enough to be a father, so she said, "What if you went missing and your father or mother had no idea whether you were dead or alive. Can you imagine how they'd feel?"

Jay looked over his shoulder, scanning the empty desks behind him. "I don't know. If this gets out, I could lose my job, or worse. You promise not to use my name?"

"Promise."

"The day the boy disappeared, two officers came into the station with evidence sealed in bags. They asked me to log it into the evidence room, which I did."

"What evidence?"

"A bottle of grape juice, a Red Sox baseball cap, and an empty prescription bottle. Oh, and a small rug. I logged the items in carefully. Since I was new, I pulled up the instructions and followed them to the letter so I wouldn't make a mistake."

"And then what?"

"The next day when I was retrieving something from the evidence room related to another case, I noticed the items were gone. I double checked to make sure they hadn't been moved, but they were gone."

"Did you ask someone where they went?"

"I checked the log, and the entries I'd made the day before had disappeared. Later that day, two of the guys I worked with were gone. Fired? Transferred? No one would say. They were the ones who brought in the items. I kept my mouth shut. There's not a day I don't wonder what happened to the evidence, the officers, and the boy."

Emily said, "I'm hoping my new book turns up some answers. If not, it will hopefully draw attention to the case once again. Thanks for your help."

"Hope you find that little boy. Remember, don't use my name."

"I got you. And I'll send you a copy of my book when it comes out."

When they got back to the car, Emily said, "Do you remember how to get to Mair's?"

"I do, but do you want to stop and get a bite to eat first? We passed a pizza place on the way into town."

Maddy said, "I'm starving."

Emily was anxious to go back to Mair's but went along with the consensus. She was more convinced than ever that Mair was responsible for Nathan's death. Nathan's father also mentioned the juice, and the missing rug. He'd also told her Mair took prescription sleep medication. Mair was the only one with a motive.

After all, how many enemies does a twelve-year-old boy make?

The pizza place was across the street from the historic museum, which was now closed. Henry easily found a parking space out front. As soon as they entered, they were greeted by a hostess in a tiger costume, who handed them off to a waitress dressed like Mulan.

"Want to share a veggie pizza?" asked Maddy. She had to repeat the question before Emily answered.

"Huh? I'm sorry, I was thinking about the missing evidence." Mair's father had to know she was guilty. Otherwise, why would he have cared about getting rid of the items. "Veggie pizza sounds great."

"Don't you think whoever took the evidence must have destroyed it by now?" said Henry.

"Probably, but maybe if we search the barn and servants' quarters we'll find something. Nathan's father said an area rug was missing. I'm thinking she used it to carry the body and had to have hidden it. Her husband would have noticed it thrown in the trash or out on the porch. I was thinking, maybe she buried Nathan in it. I wonder if the police ever dug up the barn floor."

"From what we've heard, Mair's father wouldn't have authorized it if he knew the body was hidden there."

"She had to have help carrying the body. It had to be her old boss I'll bet."

The waitress set the steaming hot pizza on the table. The cheese oozed from under the green peppers and mushrooms. Now, Emily's appetite kicked in. Emily's back was to the window. "Maddy, what are you looking at out that window? Trick-or-treaters?"

"No. I just had this crazy idea while staring at the museum. Henry, didn't you say Vermont was on the side of the slaves? That the underground railroad went through here?"

"That's what my parents said, and there was an exhibit in the museum showing replicas of the places the slaves hid."

"And we found a real, live tunnel at Coralee's." Emily wiped sauce from her hand.

"And Mair's house had that historic plaque on it, right?"

Emily's eyes widened. "Maddy, you're brilliant! Are you thinking there were underground rooms or tunnels in Mair's house?"

"It fits in historically." Maddy took a big bite of pizza, then wiped cheese off her chin with the red cloth napkin.

Henry summoned Mulan. "Check, please. And we'll take a box."

Chapter 28

An orange moon lit the night sky, a perfect backdrop for Halloween night. On the way to Mair's, they passed a roadside haunted house, and a pickup truck, back filled with hay, offering 'ghost rides.' Emily wondered how Maddy's classmates were celebrating Halloween tonight and if she was feeling left out. If so, she was hiding it well. She was bubbly with excitement over snooping around for slave tunnels.

"Her car is gone," said Emily. "We should park around the back of the property and go it on foot."

Henry tucked the Jeep in between a clump of evergreens near the barn. "Something tells me the barn is the place to start."

When they got to the barn door, it was closed with a rusty padlock. Henry pulled on it to no avail.

"Let me try," said Maddy. She looked around the ground. "I need something like a piece of wire."

Emily touched her hair. "I have a bobby pin." She'd been trying to grow out her bangs and had been pinning them back when they felt extra annoying. Maddy took it and pulled it straight, then stuck it in the lock.

"Are you picking the lock? How did you learn that?" said Emily.

"Back in Chicago, there was this boy I was friends with since kindergarten. He was into spy stuff and taught me how to pick a lock. Let's see if I remember."

She fumbled with the bobby pin, trying to fit it into the lock. "This isn't going to work. It's too flimsy. Do you have anything else we could use?"

Henry said, "Let me check the Jeep."

Emily shivered. It felt like a true winter night, minus the snow. She pulled a pair of gloves out of her pocket. "Maddy, do you want to borrow my scarf?"

"I'm okay. Chicago was much worse than this, especially when the wind picked up."

Henry ran back to the barn. "I found this in the glove compartment." He showed them an ultra-thin mini screwdriver. "We had an eyeglass repair kit in there. My old sun glasses kept losing the little side screw. I forgot to take it out after I replaced the glasses."

Maddy pulled off her mitten and took it in her hand. "This is perfect!"

Emily and Henry watched her fumble with the lock, turning the screw driver until the lock popped open. "Voila."

Maddy pulled at the rusty door, but it took all three of them to slide it open as it screeched from years of inertia. When they walked in, Maddy let out a blood curling scream. A swarm of bats swooped down from the rafters causing all three to cover their heads and hit the floor.

Henry put his arm around her. "It's okay. I think they're all out adding to the Halloween ambience by now. Are you alright?"

Maddy was shaking. "I guess so. I don't want to wind up with rabies or something."

Henry pulled a small flashlight from his pocket. "This was in the glove compartment also. Stay here." He slowly shone the light up over the rafters and into the corners. Then he walked across the length of the barn kicking away rotted hay and searching for critters. "I think the coast is clear." He opened one of the two horse stalls and felt along the floor. Finding nothing, he did the same in the other stall. "No false bottoms here."

Meanwhile, Emily carefully climbed the shaky ladder to the loft, feeling the walls and checking the ceiling with the flashlight on her phone. "I don't see anything here. Maddy, do you see anything down there?"

Maddy methodically crisscrossed the floor, stamping her foot and listening for hollow sounds. "Nope."

Henry dusted off his hands. "Let's move on. How about the silo?"

Maddy once again was able to pick the lock and gain entrance to the silo. It was easy to explore given it had long ago stopped storing grain. Convinced it was a dead end, they moved on to the servant's quarters, gaining access through a broken window.

"I'll check the walls; Maddy, check the floor. Emily, take my flashlight and scan every inch of the ceiling." When Emily shone the flashlight at the ceiling, a bat swooped down and made its way out the window. Her heart pounded.

Maddy covered her head for a moment, then stomped across the floor. Suddenly, she screamed even louder than when they'd encountered the bats. Henry ran over to her.

"What's wrong? Did you find something?"

Emily said, "Are you okay?"

"I...I." Maddy pointed to the corner.

"It's only a rat," said Henry. "He's more afraid of you than you are of him."

"I'm ready to go home," said Maddy.

"Okay," said Henry. "I think this is a dead end. Let's go." He put his arm around Maddy and they walked toward the car.

As they approached the evergreens, Emily stopped in her tracks. She shone her flashlight up and down around the trees. "Something's not right."

"What's the matter?" said Henry.

"Come on, Emily. I don't want to run into more bats."

"Wait, Maddy. Both of you, look at that tree back there. Does it look weird to you?"

Henry walked closer to it. "It's rotted out, except at the bottom of the trunk, it's not." He shone the light and touched the tree. "It's not even wood. It's metal, painted to look like wood." He pushed on the trunk, feeling for a handle or some way to open it.

"Push up from the bottom," said Maddy. "Like you open a garage door." An owl hooted and she jumped. "Hurry, I want to get out of here."

Henry pushed from the bottom, and the rusty door slipped up into the rotted trunk. "I think we found something!" He shone the light. "It's some sort of tunnel, just barely big enough to crouch through." He started to go in.

Emily grabbed his arm. "Henry, it could be dangerous. What if it collapses on you?"

"What if there are rats in there?" said Maddy.

Henry came back out. "You're right. Even more, if there's a body hidden there, we want the police to find it with a search warrant so they can use it in court. Come on. We'll stop back at the station and talk to Jay Hart. He should still be there, right?"

"He mentioned having to be there until midnight. Let's go."

"Wait. If we go to him, he'll know we were trespassing. I have a better idea. Give me your phone." He scrolled to the number of the police station. "Officer, I'd like to report a break in…"

Chapter 29

Emily could barely look at Mair at work the next day. She was dying to know what happened when the Oakbridge police checked Mair's property after their anonymous call about the break in last night. She half expected them to be at St. Edwards this morning, arresting her.

"Did Maddy have a good Halloween?" asked Nancy. Emily was so lost in her own thoughts, she hadn't realized Nancy was behind her.

"I think so. What about Brooke? Did she go trick-or-treating or are they too old for that?"

"They aren't too old. Brooke went around with a few friends from school, then they came back to our house and binged on chocolate. Brooke invited Maddy but she didn't want to join them."

Emily looked around the mailroom. "Have you seen Mair yet?"

"Speak of the devil," said Nancy. Mair strutted in, barking orders. "Remember to take attendance first thing. I don't want you accepting any lame excuses about being late or missing class because of Halloween, you hear me?"

Did she miss something? Was this college or elementary school? Emily wondered if she was really expecting a 'Yes, Ma'am' from her staff. Maybe a salute to go with it. It'd be a cold day in Hell before she'd get either from her.

All through her first class, Emily peeked out the window for a cruiser and listened for sirens. Nothing.

She was disappointed, and wondered if the police hadn't found anything. Perhaps they'd gotten all excited over nothing. Just because they'd found a secret tunnel, it didn't mean Mair hid her dead son in it.

Emily's phone rang at lunch time. It was Henry.

"Any news? Did they come to the school to pick up Mair?"

"Nada."

"Maybe they just need to get all their ducks in a row before they can make an arrest. Let me know if you hear anything. I'll see you at dinner time."

Emily washed down her almond butter sandwich with a can of Diet Dr. Pepper. Nancy peeked into her office. "Coming?"

She grabbed her bag and walked with Nancy to the lecture hall, where her students were waiting with open laptops. Emily couldn't focus. While trying to lecture, she kept daydreaming about Mair in handcuffs doing a walk of shame in front of all the staff and students. She listened for sirens and continually peeked out the window. Before she knew it, class was over. Disappointed, she went back to her office to lock up and grab her things.

Nancy met up with her on the way. "You okay?"

"Fine, just tired and anxious to get home."

"Me, too. Let's blow this pop stand."

When they got to the parking lot, she heard it. Sirens. Lots of them.

"What's going on?" said Nancy.

Emily's heart fluttered. "Let's stick around and see."

After a short wait, Emily got her happy ending. She and Nancy, as well as everyone else still on campus, watched the police walk a handcuffed Mair, covering her face with a jacket, into the police car, pushing down her head as she got into the back seat.

On the way home, she called Henry to tell him what had just transpired. When she got home, he had the local news on the TV and Maddy was sitting beside him on the sofa.

"Emily, they found a body! They haven't officially identified it, but you know it has to be Nathan. They said on the news that the police received an anonymous report of a break-in on the property last night and when they went to investigate, they found a tunnel which led back to the main house. That's where they found the body."

Emily's phone rang. "It's Mair's ex—Nathan's father."

"Mrs. Fox, I want to thank you. Somehow, your interest in my son's case led to the discovery of his body."

"I can't take credit. It's the Oakbridge police who found him. I'm so sorry for your loss," said Emily.

"In my heart, I knew he was dead. At least I have closure and that witch Mair will be punished. I want the public to know all the details about the horrible thing she did to her own son. You're still writing the book, right?"

"Of course. And it will be dedicated to the memory of Nathan Rose."

Emily relaxed into the sofa next to Maddy. "I'm glad justice was done. We did it!" She high-fived Maddy and Henry.

Henry said, "That's not the only piece of good news today. I heard from the lawyer. We're on track to legally adopt Maddy. We have a court date and everything. We'll be a family before the holidays." He hugged Maddy, and Emily did the same.

"Oh, and more good news," said Maddy. "Abby called. She finished the mural. And I called the Humane Society. They're bringing six cats over on Saturday morning to Coralee's. Coralee says the café is nearly set to go. Noah and Franklin are finishing up some furniture and have already set up the cat condo."

"Now, if we could just solve Danielle's murder, all the loose ends would be tied up," said Emily. "Let's make dinner. We have leftover pizza from yesterday and I'll throw together a salad."

After dinner, Emily sat at her laptop and worked on the new book until well past midnight. She managed to get out for an early run the next morning, then off to work. It was the first time all semester she didn't feel as if a weight dropped on top of her when she pulled into the parking lot at St. Edwards. Now, she could enjoy teaching again.

The entire mailroom buzzed with gossip over Mair's arrest. The mood was a mix of horrified over what Mair had done, and celebratory over the fact that she was gone. Even the students couldn't stop talking about it. During class, Emily diverted from her planned lesson and instead talked about writing true crime books, which is what she'd originally intended as the focus of this class before Mair thwarted her plans.

When she got home, Henry was on the phone with Pat. Maddy was in her room doing homework.

"Then she's close?" said Henry. "He fits the description and doesn't have an alibi for the night Danielle was killed? Maybe this town will see two murders resolved this week. See you Saturday, buddy."

"Megan found Charles Wilkerson?"

"Yep. And he's looking good as a suspect."

"Any news on Mair?"

"Full confession. Don't you watch the news? She was tired of dealing with an autistic son, wanted to run off with her old boss, who didn't want children, and took things into her own hands. She drugged Nathan, played a game of hide and seek with him, and left him in the tunnel to die. She threw the rug into the tunnel because Nathan spilled grape juice on it. End of story."

"She worked alone, then?"

"Yep. Didn't need the help of her ex-boss. He claims he had no intention of leaving his wife and hooking up with her and that she was a nut case. Oh, and they arrested Mair's father for tampering with evidence."

"I'm so glad the truth finally came out, even though it doesn't bring Nathan back."

"At least Nathan's father can bury his son now."

Chapter 30

"Maddy, you have to eat something. If you don't want oatmeal, at least grab a piece of toast."

"Emily, I'm too excited to eat. Besides, we can get something later. I can't believe it's really happening. In just a few hours, Coralee's Cozy Cat Café will be open for business."

"Henry and I are so proud of you. That's quite an accomplishment getting your project up and running so quickly." Emily scooped out a bowl of oatmeal and poured herself a cup of coffee.

"The colleges are going to be impressed," said Henry. "And when it's time to apply for veterinary school, you can show a long history of interest in helping animals."

"That's like, eight years away, but whatever. I'm going to get in the shower."

"The press will be there," said Emily. "You should wear that cute velvet dress we ordered from Amazon."

"A dress? Whatever." Maddy grabbed Chester and headed to her room.

Henry looked up from the newspaper. "Mair's father confessed to tampering with evidence and was charged with obstructing justice. He's going to lose his pension and is looking at jail time."

"He's getting what he deserved. The apple didn't fall far from the tree, did it?"

"Speaking of apples and trees, I was thinking we can throw a party after our court date to celebrate Maddy's adoption."

"That's an excellent idea. Maybe we can do a family trip as well. How about Disneyworld during Christmas break? The weather will be nice in Florida, and the parks will be decked out for the holidays. I wonder if she's ever been?"

"Let's surprise her at her adoption party. It'll be our first gift to her as parents."

Emily finished breakfast, loaded the dishwasher, and jumped in the shower. Henry finished the Sudoku, then received a text from the lawyer handling the adoption. They had a court date. The adoption hearing was scheduled for the Friday before Thanksgiving. As anxious as he was to run and tell Emily and Maddy, he restrained himself. He didn't want to detract from the excitement of the grand opening. He'd share the news tonight.

Maddy, looking like an antique China doll in her burgundy dress, came into the kitchen. "Come on. I don't want to be late."

Henry put on a suit jacket, and Emily came in wearing a winter white pant suit.

"I have to say, this is one good-looking family," said Henry. "I'm going to ask Abby to take a family picture in front of the inn."

The air was brisk and the sky a steely gray. Emily tucked her scarf around her neck and watched Maddy zip her ski jacket over her elegant dress. Next weekend she'd take her to buy a proper winter coat to wear with dress clothes.

They got into the Jeep and headed to Coralee's.

"Look at all the cars already!" said Maddy. The front lot of the inn was completely full.

In front of the inn, Emily spotted the local news van. A familiar reporter stood outside testing a microphone. Henry pulled around back and parked near the kitchen entrance. Coralee, busy overseeing the gala, greeted them.

"This is already turning out to be fabulous! Everyone's waiting for you to cut the ribbon, Maddy. I even set out a little podium—you've got to make a speech!"

Coralee led them through the crowd to the new café. A hand-painted sign hung over the door, and a blue ribbon guarded the entrance. The reporter who had been outside, was poised with her camera man beside her. When the crowd saw Maddy, they clapped and whistled. Coralee took the podium.

"We are delighted to see such an enthusiastic turnout for Sugarbury Falls' one and only cat café. As you know, all profits are going to support the Humane Society right here in town. Hopefully, some of you will leave with a new feline friend, but even if you are unable to give a cat a home, please enjoy their company and spread the word to your friends. Now, I'd like to introduce the young lady who made all this possible. Maddy Fraser."

Maddy worked her way to the podium. Emily whispered in Henry's ear. "Coralee doesn't know Maddy's last name. You don't think Maddy will want to take our last name after she's adopted, do you?"

"I think that's too much to hope for. She'll want to keep Fiona's family name alive, knowing Maddy."

Henry and Emily both knew Maddy hated speaking in front of crowds and were pleasantly surprised at her ease as she took her spot to speak.

"I'm touched that we have so many cat lovers amongst us. This started as a school project, but has become a true passion. I'd like to thank everyone who made today possible, from the people who showed up to paint, Noah and Franklin who built the cat furniture, my school counselor, Mrs. Richards, the Humane

Society of Sugarbury Falls, Coralee, of course, and most especially, my parents, Emily and Henry Fox for believing in this project and helping me from the start."

Emily wiped a tear from her eye and squeezed Henry's hand.

Cameras snapped photos, the crowd clapped, and the reporter asked a few questions before letting Maddy leave the podium. Then, Coralee handed Maddy the scissors.

"Go on, Maddy. Cut the blue ribbon. You should be the first to enter."

Maddy walked inside, smiling from her hair to her toes. Emily and Henry stood beside her, beaming with pride.

The café was painted light green with white trim. A mural of every imaginable type of cat covered one wall, opposite the giant cat condo. Baskets of donated cat toys flanked cushy chairs, a sectional sofa, and several tables that Henry made in his barn workroom. A glass partition separated the food preparation area from the cats, but once the food was purchased, guests were free to carry it into the cat room. Henry snapped pictures with his phone.

Most of the cats hid when bombarded with all the people, but eventually some found their way to laps. A steady stream of people passed through the café and nearly all the cats were adopted, though the Humane Society assured everyone there were plenty more coming. Maddy collapsed into a chair next to Emily and Henry, holding Max on her lap. He was most definitely not up for adoption. The door flung open.

"Excuse me. Excuse, me. I'm looking for Maddy Fraser." Max jumped down off Maddy's lap and hid under a chair.

Henry wondered if he was another reporter. "Here's the lady of the day right here."

"Great. Come here, Maddy. I've been searching for you. It's me." He ran to Maddy and gave her a bear hug.

Henry put his arm on the man, releasing his grip on Maddy. "Don't grab my daughter like that."

"Your daughter? I'm afraid there's been a mistake. I came to bring Maddy home. I'm her uncle, Fiona's brother. Don't you remember me, Maddy? It's Uncle Malcolm!"

Chapter 31

Exhausted and feeling like she'd been hit with a steel beam, Emily went into her kitchen, spilled water as she poured it into the Keurig, then dropped coffee grinds all over the counter. Out of the blue, after all these months, an uncle pops up, wanting to take Maddy back to Scotland to live with him. Where was he all this time? And if Fiona trusted him, surely she would have named him guardian instead of her. She felt like her heart was being twisted and wrung out like a wet towel, leaving her limp and breathless.

Henry wanted to punch the interloper who showed up just at the moment Maddy was about to become their daughter. Instead, he made polite chit-chat while Emily made coffee. Maddy sat beside him on the couch, her head leaning against his upper arm.

Henry cleared his throat. "So, what brings you here now, so many months after your sister's death?"

"Aye, a good question indeed. I'd been traveling, out on safari in Africa. Shoulda seen the rhinoceros I shot. Bam, right between his eyes. Got a Bengal tiger as well. He's at the taxidermist, but will be sitting pretty over my mantle by Christmas."

Maddy turned pale, then excused herself. Henry followed. Hearing her throw up in the guest bathroom, he felt helpless, wanting to grab her and make everything okay.

"Maddy, are you going to be alright?"

"I'm not going with him. He kills animals? On purpose? I hate him already and I sure don't want to move to Scotland. Don't I get a say in this?"

Henry felt sick. "I'm going to call a lawyer the minute he leaves. If he thinks he's going to take you away from us, he'd better brace for a fight." He heard Emily talking in the living room. "I'm going to get back there and see if I can make sense out of his story. You don't have to join us if you're not up to it."

Henry noticed Emily's hand shaking as she handed Malcolm a mug of coffee. He could tell she'd gone into reporter mode, trying to put together this bizarre story.

"So, you were in Africa when Fiona died. When had you last spoken to her? She barely mentioned you when we were roommates back in college."

"We lost track of each other. I worked undercover for Scotland Yard for years and went long stretches where I was forbidden to contact my family, for their own safety. I couldn't put my own sister or my little niece in danger."

Emily thought he looked a bit too old to have just recently retired, especially from such a physical job. She felt her face heat up with anger. "You retired when?"

"When I felt the time was right. I have return plane reservations for me and the girl on Tuesday. Whatever she can't pack, you can send later."

Emily's heart sank. "That's too soon. Maddy is in the middle of the quarter at her school and she just launched her community service project. If you care about her, you won't rip her away. She's barely adjusted here after having to leave Chicago when her mother died."

"There's a first-class prep school not far from my home. She'll be just fine. Now, I think I'd best be getting back to the inn. Jet lag is a bear. I'll be back tomorrow to visit with my niece."

Henry locked the door behind him. Emily screamed, "I'm not letting him take her. Call a lawyer."

Henry fumbled with his phone. "Do you have a lawyer in mind?"

"No. Don't you know anyone at the hospital who can recommend someone? What about Pat?"

Henry said, "One of the nurses in the emergency room is married to a lawyer. I'll try her."

Meanwhile, Emily knocked on Maddy's door. Getting no response, she gently pushed the door open and saw Maddy crying on the bed, Chester cradled under her arm. She wanted to sound strong and comforting, but instead, broke into sobs as she sat on the bed next to Maddy.

"He can't just take me, can he? I'll run away before I go with him. He could be a pedophile for all we know. I'm not getting on a plane with a stranger and I'm not leaving my home." She buried her face in the pillow.

Emily couldn't stop the tears and her voice broke as she spoke through them. "Henry's getting in touch with a lawyer right now. There has to be something we can do."

She laid next to Maddy, unable to think clearly. Just when they were about to become a family, a stranger threatened to shatter their lives. Why would he want the responsibility of raising a teenager when he had the freedom to travel and do as he pleased? Something didn't feel right.

Henry walked in, phone still in hand. "I talked to the nurse's husband. He's a tax lawyer, but he referred me to a friend of his. We're going to meet with him first thing in the morning. Maddy, are you sure your mom had no contact with this uncle of yours? Did she ever talk about him?"

"I haven't heard his name since I was maybe, five or six years old. If she trusted him, wouldn't she have made him my guardian? Obviously she wanted me to live with Emily."

Emily said, "She named me your guardian years ago. What if she changed her mind?"

Henry said, "If she had, surely she would have amended the paperwork. Let's take a deep breath and wait to see what the lawyer says."

Emily went to bed early, but tossed and turned, debating whether or not to get out of bed and watch television.

"I can't sleep, either," said Henry. "I love Maddy. She'll be miserable if he takes her away. Remember what happened when we were deciding whether or not to accept custody right after Fiona died?"

"How could I forget? She took all those pills she got her hands on at her foster home. She'll try that again, won't she?" Emily grabbed a tissue from her nightstand.

"I like to think she's much stronger now, but I question why Malcolm wants her? He didn't look at her with any sort of affection."

"Maddy looks just like Fiona. If it were you and you met your dead sister's child for the first time, wouldn't you say something like she reminded you of her?"

"He barely talked about Fiona, as a matter of fact."

"And do you buy that whole story about Scotland Yard and the safari?"

"I'm not taking his word for it. I'll talk to Megan after we see the lawyer and see if she can do some kind of background check."

"Better yet," said Emily. "I know someone close to home who can help us."

Chapter 32

In the morning, the first snowfall of the season blanketed the roads. Henry and Emily drove silently to the lawyer's office.

"Thank you for coming in on a Sunday," said Henry.

The lawyer said, "It sounded urgent. Hope I can help. Have a seat. Can I get you some coffee?"

Anxious to get started, they both shook their heads. Emily spit out the whole story, barely stopping to breathe.

"Do you have the guardianship letter?"

"It's in the safe at home."

The lawyer scribbled notes on a yellow legal pad. "First, we have to get a background check. If he's ever been in trouble with the law, we can make a case."

"And if he hasn't?" asked Emily.

"The courts favor blood relatives, but let's take it one step at a time. Do you have access to Maddy's school records?"

"I can get them," said Emily.

"Make a list of people who have witnessed interactions between the two of you and Maddy. People who are willing to vouch for the three of you as a family."

Emily started a list in her head...Kurt, Megan, Pat, Nancy, Coralee...

"If you sign this permission form, I'll access her medical records. We want to show Maddy is well taken care of, in good health, and emotionally sound. Has she ever been to a counselor or therapist?"

"You mean a psychologist?" said Henry.

"Yes, or even a guidance counselor who can attest to the fact that Maddy has adjusted well to living in Sugarbury Falls with the two of you."

"We probably can, but he's planning on taking her back to Scotland in two days."

"I understand, Mr. Fox. We'll work as rapidly as possible. Even if he does get her on that plane..."

Emily jumped up. "What do you mean *if*? He can't get her on the plane, I thought you understood that."

"Calm down, Mrs. Fox. All I'm saying, is if we run out of time before we get our ducks in a row, Scotland law won't block us from bringing Maddy back if the court decides to deny custody to Maddy's uncle."

Henry squeezed Emily's hand. "Thank you. Let us know if you need anything further."

Back in the Jeep, Emily said, "He's been with Scotland Yard his whole career. What are the chances he has a criminal record? If we don't find something, we're going to lose our daughter. We should find another lawyer."

"I'm not going to let that happen," said Henry. His phone vibrated. "Pat, yeah, we're in the car. Just saw a lawyer. Can Megan dig up anything on Uncle Malcolm for us?"

Pat's voice came through the car's Bluetooth. "She has to go through proper channels, as she put it. It's going to take some time."

"We don't have time," said Emily. "He's taking our daughter across the ocean in two days."

"I know. I don't mean to make light of the situation. The three of you are a perfect family—even got us talking about having kids of our own one day. I called for another reason. Megan interviewed Brody's father. He doesn't have an alibi for the night of Danielle's murder. In fact, he didn't show up at work that day and the neighbor says his car wasn't in the driveway, and the newspaper was piled up on the stoop."

Emily said, "Did they check flights?"

"So far, no commercial travel, but Megan's getting toll records. Problem is, he could have taken back roads. Megan says he fits the physical description gotten from your neighbor's photo, Anyway, it's the first new lead they've had."

"Thanks, buddy. Keep us posted." Henry put his hand on Emily's thigh. "It's all going to work out."

"I'm not willing to sit back and wait. Let's make a stop on the way home."

Without having to ask, Henry drove to Rebecca and Abby's cabin. "Their cars are here. Think we should have called first?"

"I think they'll understand the urgency."

Emily took the lead. Standing on the fall inspired welcome mat, her heart raced as she knocked. Rebecca was her best shot at saving Maddy. Milo barked, and Rebecca answered the door. "I'm sorry to come by unannounced, but it's an emergency."

"Come on in. We were just hanging out, doing the Sunday puzzles. Did you see the great article about the cat café? Nice picture of Maddy with the cats. Can I get you some coffee?"

"No, thanks. Rebecca, remember the uncle who showed up at Coralee's yesterday?"

"How can I forget with that grand entrance he made."

"He wants to take Maddy back to Scotland. We talked to a lawyer, but he's a blood relative and I'm afraid we're going to lose Maddy." She wiped away tears as Henry put his arm around her.

Rebecca was no nonsense. "Let's check this guy out." She opened her computer. "Spell his name for me." Rebecca clicked the keys while Emily and Henry peered over her shoulder.

"The dude lives in an actual castle in Scotland. It's been in the family since the 1600's. Let me check something." She searched while Emily and Henry stood frozen, hopeful for information.

"You know, he's the last of the family line. It was him and Fiona, and he had no children. Looks like next in line is Maddy. When he passes on, the castle is hers."

Henry said, "So maybe he wants to bring her there to carry on his legacy after he dies. Still doesn't explain why he needs custody. She'd still inherit it, right?"

"Yes, along with quite a fortune. You said he worked at Scotland Yard? Must pay a mean pension." She tried another search. "I can't get into the Scotland Yard's employment records. Let's try education. Did your roommate ever mention where he went to college?"

"No. She barely mentioned him at all. Her mother grew up in Edinburgh, so I suppose he did as well."

Rebecca searched. "Father was a businessman, mother listed as a homemaker. One sister—Fiona."

"That's it!"

"They both went to a prep school, he went on to Cambridge, majored in business."

Amazed at the ease in which Rebecca found the information, Emily said, "If he was a businessman, how did he wind up at Scotland Yard?"

Rebecca kept going. "This is interesting."

Henry moved closer, looking over her shoulder. "He donated a ton of money to Huntington's disease research. Check out how the parents died. Huntington's is hereditary and always deadly."

Rebecca accessed death records. "Mom died of breast cancer. Father died…of Huntington's."

Henry said, "That means both children had a fifty/fifty risk of inheriting the disease. Em, did Fiona ever mention it?"

"No, I'm pretty sure I'd have remembered if she did. Do you think that's how she died?"

"It's a long progression and at the end, the person needs full time care. There's no way Fiona could have cared for Maddy if that was the case."

"Oh my God! Do you think there's a chance Maddy has it?"

"Fiona died in her mid-fifties. If she had the disease, I'm pretty sure she'd have known it by then. I can do some digging through the hospital." Henry squeezed Emily's hand.

Abby came in, hair wet from the shower. "Hey, I thought I heard voices."

Emily said, "Rebecca is amazing. She could make a fortune doing private investigating."

Abby put her hands on Rebecca's shoulders. "She sure could. We're going to a craft fair this afternoon. Want to come along?"

"No, thanks," said Emily. "We should be going. Have fun, and thanks again, Rebecca."

Chapter 33

When they got home, Maddy was watching a movie on the sofa, still in her pajamas, hair unbrushed.

"Maddy, we went to see a lawyer, and then Rebecca came up with some important information. We're not going to lose you."

"Emily, I'd rather die than go to Scotland with my uncle."

Alarms went off inside Henry's head. "You don't mean that, right?" He'd heard a story just the other day on NPR about the rise in teen suicide, and then there was the incident with the sleeping pills back in Chicago...

Maddy didn't answer.

Emily said, "Did your mom seem sick at all, before she died, I mean."

"Sick? Like how? She ran the Chicago marathon last fall. She was the healthiest person I knew—until she died."

"Did she ever mention Huntington's disease?"

"Yes. Her father died from it. Why?"

"Nothing important," said Henry. "Want to go over to the cat café later? We can have dinner there."

"Maybe."

"In fact, I'll ask Pat and Megan if they want to meet us. Megan's been investigating your uncle and if we're lucky, she may have come up with something to prevent him from taking you."

Emily sat down at her desk, but had difficulty concentrating on her writing. She and Henry were supposed to be retired. Nothing stopped them from selling their cabin and moving to Edinburgh themselves to be near Maddy! She found peace now that she had a plan for dealing with the worst case scenario. Another four years and Maddy would be eighteen and free to live where ever she wanted. Emily began to type. *For those who question whether pure evil exists in this world, the story of a mother who plotted and carried out the murder of her own son, then hid his body in a deserted tunnel beneath her house will leave you without doubt.*

Before she knew it, Henry came in. "Let's get ready. Pat and Megan are meeting us at five."

Maddy was silent in the backseat the whole ride to the inn. It got dark so early in the winter, that Emily, already depressed over the current situation, would have preferred staying home in her sweats and ordering pizza. She hoped seeing the cat café would cheer Maddy up, and that Megan might have more news to share. On the other hand, perhaps this was a terrible idea. What if seeing the cats made Maddy realize the café would go on without her and what if Megan had bad news?

Coralee stood at the entrance to the inn. "See that line? It's all for the cat café. Maddy, this is going to be big. Ten cats have been adopted since it opened yesterday."

She led them to a table in the dining room, which was opposite the cat café. "Maddy, honey, it's going to be okay. That so called uncle is up to no good. I can feel it in my bones. There's no way he'll get past our detectives and drag you across the ocean. As a matter of fact, Detective O'Leary is in there now and she told me she's working day and night to keep you here."

Maddy shrugged her shoulders and followed Henry and Emily to the table.

Pat jumped up when he saw them. "Megan can't find any record of this guy working at Scotland Yard. As a matter of fact, he's been getting disability checks from the government for years. He must be living off family money or something."

Megan said, "The castle was renovated fifteen years ago. That's when Malcolm sold his flat in the city and moved to the outskirts. The renovation cost a fortune."

"Was he married?" asked Emily.

"No marriage license issued. Also, he let his driver's license expire years ago. Maybe a chauffeur came with the castle."

Emily said, "Fiona worked her way through college, and didn't leave behind much money to care for Maddy. You're saying her family was rich?"

"Fiona's father invested in a business when Fiona must have been a baby. He left it to Malcolm. It was losing money, but a few years ago, it took off. With his business degree, Malcolm may have turned it around."

Henry said, "So, the man has a business degree, successfully turns around a business, and joins the police force? Then he goes on disability, but still manages to live in a castle? Something doesn't add up."

"He looks perfectly healthy to me," said Maddy.

"Well, some disabilities aren't visible. Not that I trust the man," said Henry.

Emily's heart dropped. Standing in the entrance was Uncle Malcolm, bundled in a tweed coat. Coralee awkwardly pointed to their table and followed as he approached their table.

"Well, I'll be. What a nice chance to get to know my niece a little better." He sat at the empty place, taking the menu out of Coralee's hand. His coat smelled of smoke and his breath reeked of whiskey. Emily completely lost her appetite.

"Just wait, little lassie. I'll take you out for a proper Scottish dinner at Dubh Prais over on High Street when we get back home. They have the best venison in the city."

Maddy made a face and shuddered.

"If you don't like venison, they have a bloody good lemon sole with cheese sauce."

Maddy looked up at him. "I don't do meat."

Henry changed the subject. "So how do you spend your days now that you're retired?"

"Hunting and fishing during the season. Reading and traveling during the winters. Do you like to read, lassie? I can take you to the Elephant House Café where that Rowlings lady wrote Harry Potter. When you go to the toilet, there are messages written all over the walls and even the windows in honor of Harry Potter."

Emily wanted to throw up, picturing Maddy surrounded by venison and a graffiti-filled bathroom with an uncle who fished and killed animals in his spare time. Distracted by her nightmarish thoughts, she accidentally cut her finger while cutting the sautéed asparagus on her plate.

Uncle Malcolm grabbed a handkerchief from his pocket and wrapped it around Emily's finger. "Direct pressure will stop the bleeding. You have to wash it out so it doesn't get infected. I assume you've had a recent tetanus shot?"

Emily yanked her hand away. "Even if I wasn't married to a doctor, I'd know that much."

Megan said, "So tell me about Scotland Yard? Must have been an exciting career."

"It had its moments. Sometimes I miss the thrill of the chase."

"When did you move to Scotland? After you retired?"

Uncle Malcolm cleared his throat. "What do you mean?"

"I mean, Scotland Yard is in London, not Edinburgh. When did you move, when you retired?"

"I did undercover work in Scotland for them. Moved out of London half a dozen years ago." Malcolm looked at the blood soaking through the handkerchief. "You may need a suture or two."

Emily said, "Yeah, I think we'll be going. I want to take care of this, and Maddy has school tomorrow. Me too, as a matter of fact." One pleasant thought in the midst of this vortex of doom was the fact that Mair Rose was in prison, and no longer at St. Edwards.

Chapter 34

When Emily pulled into St. Edwards, she was surprised that Nancy's car was already parked in the lot. She gathered her tote, and on the way in, prayed for something to turn up that would keep Maddy with them. Would Maddy survive being uprooted? The better question—would *she* recover from losing part of her family? Again?

She checked her messages and noticed a missed call from the lawyer who'd been handling Maddy's adoption. While she listened, tears streamed down her face. He was confirming their court date. By the end of the month, Maddy could officially be their daughter. She wasn't ready to call the lawyer and cancel—not yet.

Nancy ran up to her in the mailroom. "Guess what? I've been offered Mair's position! Officially I'm interim, but at least for now I can make life much more pleasant around here. And the increase in salary will really help us."

Emily hugged her. "I'm so happy for you. You're the perfect choice for the job."

Nancy's worry lines reappeared. "I'm so sorry. Here I am all happy and you must be worried sick. Any news on Uncle Malcolm?"

"Both Megan and Rebecca are working on it, but we're running out of time. I wish Fiona hadn't insisted on Maddy having a passport. That could have slowed things down. I almost told Maddy to pretend she'd lost it."

"Why don't you go home? You can reschedule your class."

"Maddy went to school today. She's trying to keep things routine for herself, though I know she's terrified."

Two other faculty members approached Nancy, offering hugs and congratulations. Emily slipped out and got ready for her class.

*****

"Pat, are you sure?" said Henry. After a busy morning in the emergency room, he met Pat in the cafeteria for lunch.

"Megan searched travel records. Uncle Malcolm didn't just arrive. He's been in town for a month!"

"She's sure? He checked into Coralee's just last Saturday."

"Yeah. He flew in from Edinburgh via JFK, then rented the white Toyota he's still driving. She has restaurant receipts, credit card charges, the whole shebang."

"Why would he sneak around a whole month before claiming Maddy?"

"She's working on it. And she contacted her buddy in London. He did some searching. There's no record of Uncle Malcolm ever working for Scotland Yard, undercover or not."

Henry picked the crust off of his grilled cheese sandwich. What was Uncle Malcolm hiding? "Fiona and Malcolm sure beat the odds if neither inherited Huntington's. Surely they were tested. If we can prove Malcolm is medically compromised and would be unable to care for Maddy..."

"That could be why he retired early—if he truly worked for Scotland Yard, but he didn't work for them, according to what Megan's found."

Henry crumbled the crust between his fingers.

"At his age, he'd already be showing symptoms, right?" said Pat.

"We don't see him 24/7. For all we know, he is." Henry's phone vibrated. "I've got to get back upstairs. Some kid was brought in with a broken arm. Keep me posted. Tell Megan thanks."

"Gotcha buddy."

Henry handled the emergency, then went to his desk. Knowing he didn't have access to medical records that weren't his patients', he mentally ran through his contacts. He had an old colleague who moved somewhere in Europe. He'd seen his name on an article in a medical journal not too long ago. He grabbed the stack of journals off his bookshelf and scanned the table of contents of each one. When he was nearly two-thirds through the stack, he found what he was looking for. He flipped through his ancient rolodex.

"Thaddeus, it's Henry Fox. I'm doing fine. Hoping we'll run into each other at another conference in the near future. The reason I'm calling, is I need emergency access to medical records for a Malcolm Fraser and I know you have universal records over there. I wouldn't ask if it wasn't an emergency. You'll try? Call me anytime. Great."

Henry checked on the last few patients in the emergency room, then headed home. It seemed proving Malcolm incompetent due to medical issues was the most direct way of blocking custody. Why did Malcolm lie about working for Scotland Yard? And if he wasn't working for them, why had he lost contact with his sister all those years? He pulled into his driveway behind Emily's car.

Emily and Rebecca were seated on the sofa, engrossed in conversation. Emily whipped around. "You have to hear this. Rebecca found something."

Henry tossed his coat on the coat rack and sat down next to them.

Rebecca showed him a printout. "Uncle Malcolm wasn't living alone in that castle. He was living with a man named Josefer Rubric."

"You mean, like they were a couple?"

"No. I mean Josefer worked for Malcolm. To make a long story short, Josefer was a nurse, hired to care for Malcolm."

"Care for him?" Henry bubbled. "So he does have Huntington's after all. Let's get Megan to talk to him. We can use him to build a case that Malcolm will soon be unable to care for Maddy."

"Hang on," said Rebecca. "There's a complication."

"What complication?" He was getting impatient and wished Rebecca would just spit out everything she knew all at once.

"Josefer is dead. Died a few months back. Malcolm's been living alone since."

"So we have another dead end," said Henry.

"Maybe not."

Again, Henry wanted to shake the words from her mouth. "Go on."

"I figured two men, one medically compromised, wouldn't be up to cleaning a castle without help, or cooking, or keeping the grounds, for that matter. I spent a bit of time with my friend Google."

Emily noticed Henry's veins swelling in his neck. "What she's trying to tell us, is that she found the name of a cleaning lady who worked for Malcolm up until the time Josefer died."

"And you talked to this cleaning lady?" Henry leaned forward, hoping to finally see how the pieces worked together.

"Not exactly."

A little more gruffly than he'd intended, Henry said, "What do you mean?"

"She quit the agency after Malcolm died. I'm trying to track her down. She didn't leave a forwarding address."

"We're running out of time. Malcolm is taking her back to Scotland tomorrow. Their flight leaves at 6 p.m."

Emily squeezed his hand and held back the flood of tears welling up behind her eyes.

Chapter 35

Neither Emily nor Henry slept at all. Maddy cried most of the night, inconsolable and refusing to pack a suitcase. Emily knew she should help prepare her for the upheaval she was about to experience, but had a hard time accepting the reality of the situation.

"Maddy, we haven't given up. You may have to get on that plane tonight, but we will be fighting to get you home and I promise we will."

Henry felt uncomfortable making that sort of promise, but knew they would fight for her with every dime and every bit of emotional energy they had. "We have some leads we're waiting on. I'm sure something's going to turn up."

Maddy cradled Chester, wiping her tears on his black fur. "What's going to happen to the cat café? What about Chester?"

Emily hugged her. "Don't worry about the cats. We'll keep an eye on the café and make sure it runs smoothly until you come back."

"I don't want to go to some dumb private school in a foreign country. It was hard enough leaving Chicago and coming here. This is worse." Maddy couldn't catch her breath through her sobs. "What if I run away?"

Henry said, "We want to play this by the book. If we don't cooperate, it'll hurt our chances of getting you back. We have no choice but to send you on that plane with him."

Emily said, "If worse comes to worst, we'll sell this place and move to Scotland with you."

"Just give us a little time to follow up on our leads, first." Henry tried to be rational. It would take time for them to sell the cabin and move overseas. Maybe Emily would have to go on ahead while he tied things up here. Then again, nothing was as important at this moment as being together as a family.

"Maddy, I have to go by the college for a quick meeting, then I'll be back," said Emily. "Henry will be here with you. Give me an hour or so." She hugged Maddy tightly, then made herself pull away to get ready to go.

After Emily left, Henry said, "I hate this as much as you do, but we have to pack your things, I'll help."

"I don't want to go and I'm not packing."

"It's just for a little while. Pack the essentials and we'll keep your room just like you leave it."

Henry's phone vibrated. "Yeah? Now? You can't get anyone else?" He slammed the phone down on Maddy's bed. "I have to go to the hospital. I'll be back as soon as I can." Regretting at the moment his decision not to fully retire, he hugged Maddy and left for the hospital.

Once he arrived, he didn't have a moment to breathe. A severe car accident had brought half a dozen patients into the ER. When he'd finally finished, he checked his phone. Pat had left several texts saying Megan was with him and wanted to talk to him. Henry ran down to the morgue, hoping she would still be there.

"Sorry, had a big mess to deal with upstairs. A little ice and these tourists don't know how to drive."

"We're expecting quite the storm later today. It's only going to get worse. For me, too," said Pat.

"Megan, did you find out something?"

"Boy, did we. Danielle LaPierre. We finished going through her things and found out she was in town to deliver something to a young lady named Maddy Fraser. You remember she was an estate lawyer, right?"

"What's that have to do with Uncle Malcolm?"

*****

Emily could barely concentrate on the road, sliding on the freezing rain, distracted by thoughts of Maddy getting on the plane. She planned on being gone an hour, but the meeting dragged on, and now the weather was making it impossible to hurry. A call came through the Bluetooth system.

"Rebecca? I'm in the car and the roads are pretty bad. Can I call you when I get home? What? No way? Are you sure?"

With the determination of a starving dog, she set her sights on home, heart pounding like a jackhammer. She couldn't wait to grab Maddy and tell her everything was going to be okay. She gripped the steering wheel so tightly that her hands were numb when she finally pulled into her driveway.

"Maddy, Henry, come quick. I have some great news!" She tossed her keys on the table.

Henry, on his phone, met her at the door and signaled her to wait, cupping his hand over his ear. Emily checked Maddy's room.

"Henry, where's Maddy?" She looked at her watch. It was too early for the limo service to have picked her up to go to the airport.

Henry put the phone in his pocket. "She's gone. I came home and there's no note, she's not answering her phone. I think she ran away."

"In this weather? How far could she have gone? I have something important to tell you."

"Me, too!"

"Rebecca called me on the way home. She located the woman who cleaned the castle. She said Malcolm was dying when she left. He had a nurse—Josefer

Rubric—and he...he told her she was no longer needed. Malcolm was at death's door when she left the castle."

"And let me guess. Josefer 'died' and Malcolm made a miraculous recovery, coming to America to fetch his niece, the sole heir to the family riches."

"Rebecca uncovered a death certificate. Malcolm died of Huntington's around six weeks ago. Josefer switched places, trying to get Maddy before anyone found out. I'll bet he planned on killing her once they got to Scotland. Thank God we found out in time."

Henry said, "We have to find Maddy."

"What if he knew we were on to him and he's taken her?" Emily opened the front door. "The storm is raging. I'm going to look for her."

"No, you can't go on foot." Henry called Megan. "The police are putting out an APB. I'm calling Coralee."

Emily pulled on her boots. Henry made his call.

"Coralee says Malcolm's airport limo just showed up, but Malcolm, I mean Josefer, is gone. I'll bet he picked Maddy up early and is on his way to JFK." He chirped open the Jeep and followed Emily out the door. "Let's head to the airport."

Emily said, "No, wait. If he took off early, that means he knew we were on to him. He wouldn't risk going to the airport."

"Canada!" said Henry. "We're so close to the border, I'll bet that's his plan." He started the car, then realized he already needed to scrape ice off the windshield.

"Hurry, Henry!" Emily turned on the heat and drummed her gloved fingers on the seat. If she could have one superpower...

Henry jumped in the seat next to her. "We're off." Thankful for four-wheel drive, he trampled over the icy roads. "I never even told you what Megan said. You won't believe it." He swerved out of the way of a tractor trailer.

"Henry, watch the road."

Pellets of ice pinged against the Jeep. Henry gripped the wheel and accelerated. "I've got this."

"What did Megan say?"

"Our Uncle Malcolm isn't only an imposter and a kidnapper. He's also a murderer."

"What!"

"When the police went through Danielle's things, they found a sealed document. It was a will, leaving the Scotland castle to Maddy. Danielle handled the transaction and was in town to deliver the news to Maddy. Malcolm, I mean Josefer, followed her here to intercept."

"So Danielle's murder had nothing to do with Splash Panels or Brody or Hartman or Winnie." The stuffy heat from the car coupled with the news made her feel nauseous. "And the whole cat commercial audition was just a coincidence."

"That's right. Maybe she volunteered to handle the transaction because she was headed here anyway, but in the end, it was all about the inheritance." Henry swerved. The storm made it nearly impossible to see, with the windshield wipers rendered useless. The desolate road was lined with snow covered pines and gradually crept up the side of a mountain.

They'd barely made it out of town when Emily shrieked, "Henry, there's a car over there on the side of the road."

Henry, wondering how she could see anything in this weather, pulled the car over to the guard rail, then got out and investigated. He wiped off the license plate with his glove. "It's a rental and it fits the description of Josefer's car. Look. It must have smashed into the guardrail." He pointed to the mangled bumper.

206 *Murder, Of Course*

"That's the white sedan that followed me. I see footprints," said Emily. She hoped she was right, but the truth was, if there were any, they were already covered by the icy snow. She found an opening through the pines. "Come on."

Emily wrapped her scarf around her nose and mouth, trying to stay warm. "There's kind of a path over here."

Henry followed her. Then he froze. "Did you hear that?"

"It's Maddy screaming. Come on!" She grabbed his hand and they followed Maddy's voice. "Look! He's just ahead." She tried to run, but fell into the snow. Henry pulled her up. She panted, "He's just ahead. Do you think you and I can take him down?"

Like a mother lion protecting her cub, she ran until she ducked behind a large tree. She whispered to Henry. "He's slowing down. He's stopping to rest. Let's go for it. On three."

Henry and Emily tackled Josefer to the ground. Maddy screamed and kicked the monster before her. Emily said, "Do you hear that?"

A beam of light illuminated the ground as the propellers whirred louder and louder.

Megan and her partner jumped out of the plane. Into her walkie, Megan said, "We got him."

Chapter 36

Henry, Maddy, and Emily snuggled on the couch under a crocheted afghan.

"Drink your hot chocolate," said Emily. "I can't believe we almost lost you."

"He was going to kill me. He said he had a change in plans and I wouldn't make it to see Scotland. I didn't think anyone would find me."

"We did and we'll be here to protect you forever," said Emily, squeezing Maddy. If the police had waited a minute longer to go after Malcolm, the helicopter would have been grounded due to the weather. They'd tell Maddy the whole story tomorrow. For now, they hugged their daughter tightly. Chester snuggled on the back of the sofa over Maddy's head, purring into her ear.

"It really does take a village, you know. Raising a child, I mean," said Emily. "If it wasn't for Megan and Rebecca, who knows how this would have played out." The wood crackled in the fireplace.

"All's well that ends well," said Henry. "And now we have a new vacation home, as long as Maddy's willing to share her castle with us."

"You mean Fiona Manor? My place outside Edinburgh?"

Henry said, "Fiona Manor. Has a nice ring to it."

Emily got up and cradled Chester in her arms. "I'm really tired. Goodnight Henry, goodnight Emily." She gave them each a kiss on the cheek and headed into her room. Before she closed the door, Maddy called back to them, "I love you."

THE END

ABOUT THE AUTHOR

 Award winning author Diane Weiner is a veteran public school teacher and mother of four grown children. Fond memories of reading Nancy Drew and Mary Higgins Clark books on snowy weekends in upstate New York inspired her to write books that would bring that kind of joy to others. Being an animal lover, she is a vegetarian and shares her home with two precious cats. In her free time, she enjoys running, shopping, attending theater productions, and spending time with her family.